MW01017371

Novels by
Robert F. Mager

Killer in Our Midst
Dying for Jade
The Reluctant Miracle Man
The Price of a Miracle
Pursuing the Steamy Novel

MAGER'S SHORTS II

▼

QUIRKY STORIES FOR THE ADVENTUROUS READER

For

Ray & Barbara

Guyll

ROBERT. F. MAGER

Enjoy!

authorHOUSE®

Cheers ...

Bob Mager

AuthorHouse™
1663 Liberty Drive
Bloomington, IN 47403
www.authorhouse.com
Phone: 1-800-839-8640

First published by AuthorHouse 10/28/2009

ISBN: 978-1-4490-3719-2 (e)
ISBN: 978-1-4490-3537-2 (sc)

Printed in the United States of America
Bloomington, Indiana

This book is printed on acid-free paper.

Aiders and Abettors

I'm always pleasantly surprised at how many people are willing to devote precious time to help scour a manuscript for boo-boos, and to make suggestions for improvement. This project was no exception.

To help identify problems *before* publication (so I'll look less like an idiot), I badgered a few adventurous and generous-hearted volunteers to point to speed-bumps they found in the stories. And a fine job they did. Like vultures hovering over an aging corpse, they picked on faulty sentences, awkward wordings, goofy plot points, and more.

You should know who they are (spirited music swells):

David Cram always gets first jab—his uncanny ability to comment on first drafts—without quenching my motivation to continue—is invaluable.

Following his initial review, Elaine Bitter, Dan Raymond, Jane Sink, Don Parks, Patty Schiano, Daniel J. Lansell, and Margaret Stewart donated their valuable time and wisdom to provide even more manuscript-smoothing insights.

Offering their unique editing skills (i.e., page-mauling with multi-colored pens) were keen-eyed Eileen Mager, and editor and writing coach Rodney L. Cron. Their scribbles and tweaks vastly improved the quality of the writing.

Finally, I owe a deep bow to master ventriloquist Nick Pawlow, and Happy, (his zombie puppet), for allowing me to use them as models in the story, "Who's the Dummy?"

To each of these stalwarts I offer my sincerest admiration and thanks for their efforts.

As always, any remaining errors and omissions are the fault of my long-suffering computer, Glitch.

R. F. Mager

Contents

POOPCORN

▼

You know how strange things happen to most people at one time or another? Well, I'm no exception. So, though what I'm about to tell you may seem a little weird, I'll just tell it the way it went down and let you make of it what you will.

I was sitting on a park bench—the park is part of my beat—stewing about not making an arrest for a whole week. If this kept up I'd never get that promotion to First Grade.

But, it was a sunny day and I had time to kill, so I wandered over to the corner snack stand to buy something to nibble on. I never could pass up the smell of freshly-popped corn, and the luscious aroma coming from Tony's stand was killing me.

So, with a fresh bag in my hand and a smile of anticipation on my face, I sauntered back to the bench under the old oak tree.

I tell you, that was the best idea I'd had all week. I wasn't getting very far with the case I was working on, and a little siesta on a park bench would be just the ticket to relax my brain.

Leaning back, I fantasized about the big case that would blast me to cop stardom, opened my bag, and popped a handful of kernels into my mouth. Yum-yum.

"Hi."

Y'know, I honestly thought I heard someone say something, but when I looked around, there wasn't anyone there.

"Hi."

There it was again. A squeaky voice sounding like it said, "Hi." I swiveled my head again but there still wasn't anyone there. This was getting a little weird. Sure, there was this squirrel squatting on the other end of the bench, but—wait a minute—could it be …?

I looked around to make sure nobody was close enough to hear, then said, "Did you say something?" I mean, I was feeling pretty foolish about then. If the guys down at the precinct caught me talking to a squirrel, they'd haul my ass off to the funny farm.

"Several times," the squirrel chirped. "You hard of hearing?"

"Are … are you really talking?" I tell you, I was pretty freaked about talking to a squirrel, if that's what I was doing. I still wasn't sure.

"You see anybody else? How about pungling up a few of those nose-tingling kernels?"

He hopped over, sat on my knee, and stuck his nose into my popcorn. Just like that.

I sat there a little stunned at the pushy squirrel helping himself like he owned the whole bag. Not that I minded all that much, it's just that I was getting a little rattled at the absurdity of the situation.

"Good grub," the squirrel squeaked. "Have some."

Talk about nerve! *Now* he was offering me some of my own popcorn.

"Go ahead," he urged. "It's really good today."

So there we sat, both nibbling from the same bag as though it were an everyday event. I pinched myself in case I'd dozed off and this was one of those zany dreams I sometimes have. But it hurt when I squeezed, so I decided I was still awake.

"Needs more salt," the squirrel said. "Got any?"

"Of course not! How come you speak English?"

"How come *you* speak English?" the critter shot back.

That stopped me for a minute. I mean, talking to a squirrel was crazy enough, but getting into an argument with one made me wonder about my sanity.

"Now look here, squirrel, I—"

"Squinky."

"What?"

"Squinky. My name. We might as well be civilized about this."

"Or?"

"Or I'll call my family—they're up there in the branches—and they'll come down and turn this yummy popcorn into poopcorn."

That took the wind out of my sails. "What's poopcorn?"

"Zheesh. You know what *poop* is, don'cha?" He lifted his butt and waggled it at me as he spoke.

"Oh, okay, I get it. Sorry … uh … Squinky. I'm not used to talking with squirrels."

"Yeah, I can see that."

"So how come you talk?"

"I learned, same as you."

"You're putting me on. How?"

"Correspondence course."

Now I knew I was losing it. A talking squirrel was hard enough to swallow, but one that *reads*, too?

"That's not possible," I said. "You'd have to be able to read to do that."

"So? My Dad, Squarky, teaches me. Reads to me every day."

"That's silly. There's no library around here, and I don't see any reading matter lying around."

"Oh, yeah? Take a closer look. There's gum wrappers, candy wrappers, soda cans, old newspapers over there in the trash can … all kinds of stuff to read."

He had me there. As I struggled to think of a suitable riposte, I noticed a woman sauntering in our direction.

"That's pretty gross," she said, eyeing the two of us eating from the same bag. "I mean, I often eat along with my doggies, but never from the same bowl."

"Racist!" Squinky said.

"Now don't be rude," I shot back.

"Oh my," the woman said. "It squeaks. And you understand what it says?"

Quick as a flash, I deduced that though I could understand Squinky, she couldn't. "I just pretend that I do." No need complicating things by explaining the unexplainable. "It passes the time." Care to join us?

As she settled onto the bench, Squinky suddenly leaped onto my shoulder, kind of agitated like, and said, "Watch out. You know who she is? Her boyfriend is cooking crack over in that yellow house across the park. She's waiting for him to bring her some to sell."

I looked her over as she nervously strangled a hankie. She was about thirty, dark hair, and seemed attractive. I couldn't tell whether she had a nice face, because the scarf around her neck hid it pretty well.

"You live in that yellow house over there?"

She whipped her head around to look at me. "How did you know?"

Without thinking, I said, "The squirrel told me." *Damn!* She must think I'm loopy as a drunken cat. "I mean, it seems logical."

She jumped up, and started to pace. "I don't know what to *do*," she blurted. "My boyfriend is cooking crack in my kitchen and I can't make him stop. I'm afraid he's going to burn my house down and—"

"She's lying!" Squinky said. "He's cooking all right but, like I said, she's waiting for him to bring her a batch to peddle."

"How do you know that?" I shot back, again forgetting who I was talking to.

"Look across the street. See that guy going into the yellow house?"

"Yeah. So?"

"He shows up every day. Probably another of their distributors. Hurry up—do something before they get away."

"Wait a minute," I protested. "How come you know so much about it?"

"Hey, you think we just sit up in the tree all day throwing nuts and pooping on bench-sitters?"

I thought about that for a split second. "No, I suppose not."

"So get going!"

If the squirrel were wrong, I might be facing a false arrest charge and be the laughing stock of the precinct for years. But, what the hell! Squinky had an honest face. The woman had started to pace again, so I stood and slapped a handcuff on her wrist.

"What—what are you *doing*?" she demanded.

"You're under arrest," I told her. "Drug dealing, and maybe other things as well." I pushed her down and manacled her wrist to the iron bench. "If you keep squirming like that, I'll handcuff your other hand, too."

She squirmed anyway, so I cuffed her other wrist to the far end of the bench.

"Oh, this is just peachy," Squinky said, hopping onto her lap and scaring the bejeezus out of her.

"Squinky, think you could call your buddies down to keep an eye on her while I call this in?" By now I was feeling like part of the family.

The pushy animal hollered something in "Squirrel" and pretty soon half a dozen of the

7

chattering critters surrounded the distraught woman.

"Don't move," I told her. "If you do, my little friends will attack and cover you with poopcorn." I dropped what was left of the bag into her lap. Since she was handcuffed with her arms spread there was no way she could get into the remnants. Besides, I thought it might do her good to have a lapful of hungry animals.

I punched numbers into my cell. When the desk sergeant came on the line, I told him, "I need a SWAT team to raid a crack house I'm watching. The perp's in there cooking as we speak."

"How do you know that?"

Well now, I couldn't just tell him a little squirrel told me, could I? "I got it from one of my snitches. Hurry up, before they blow up the place."

"Okay, but we may need your snitch to help us establish probable cause. Have him handy when the SWATs get there."

Crap. I couldn't show up with a squirrel on my shoulder, especially one that talks. "I'll do what I can," I waffled, and hung up.

When I stood and began to walk away, my collar got really agitated and shouted, "Hey, you can't leave me here with all these vicious animals."

I thought I heard some high-pitched tittering when she called the little fellas vicious. "Behave yourself and you'll be just fine. Besides, if your boyfriend is going to blow up the place you'll be better off in jail for a few days." I went over to meet the squad and tell 'em which house to hit. But the minute I turned my back, the little devils leaped on her lap and began fighting over the dregs of the popcorn.

She screamed, probably because a bunch of sharp squirrel claws were digging into her thighs as they fought for traction. When they finished what was left of the popcorn they started crawling all over her body looking for more. She screamed some more and struggled to get loose. She shut up, though, as soon as she saw the cop cars arriving with their lights flashing.

When I got back to the bench a few minutes later, she wasn't moving. It was easy to see why. The squirrels were arranged all around the bench and squeaked up a storm every time she crossed her legs or something. I un-cuffed her and marched her across the park while reciting her rights, and stuffed her into a squad car. I was mighty relieved when nobody asked to talk to my "snitch."

What I didn't realize at the time was that six nosy squirrels had followed us across the park, single file, to watch the action. I got some pretty funny looks from the SWAT guys, along with some snide remarks, like "Where'd you get the posse?" Things like that.

But "action" wasn't what the little buggers were interested in at all. When I finally caught on, I marched them over to Tony's stand and bought them each a bag of popcorn. It was the least I could do, seeing as how they solved a case I didn't even know I had, and would make me "Hero for a Day" down at the precinct.

Turned out even better than that. My own furry little posse made me a deal—felons for popcorn. That's worked out so well I've made ten major arrests in only two weeks. At that rate, I'll probably make Detective First Class before long. Not only that, I'm learning to speak "Squirrel." All for a few bucks of popcorn each day. Oh, yes, and NO poopcorn!

ANOTHER POINT OF VIEW

▼

Pointing a gnarled finger toward the silver-haired man coming out of the dilapidated store, the old woman tightened the tattered shawl around her shoulders and nudged the man standing in line behind her.

"See that old man? When he went in there, he was all bent over and walked with a cane. *Now* look at 'im. Straight as a rod and frisky as a puppy dog's tail."

The man straightened his black-and-red silk tie and flicked an imaginary speck of dust from his dark, pin-striped suit. "May I ask why *you're* here?"

The frail woman looked up and lifted her splinted left arm. "It's me arm. Broke it fallin' down the cellar stairs, I did. I'm here to get it made good as new." She paused, then asked, "You ain't never been here before?"

"No. This is my first time. I'm curious to know what this is all about."

"What it's about is the doc in there can fix whatever ails you. Free, too. No charge. Course, a donation is always welcome. I s'pose he has to pay the rent an' all."

They shuffled forward with the slowly moving line. "It wasn't always like this," the woman said. "Used to be just a few folks sittin' in the waitin' room. Never had to wait more'n half an hour. I guess now word's got 'round, the whole world is waitin' to git in."

The dapper man, now almost at the waiting-room door, turned to glance at those in line behind him. "What's he like?"

"'Bout average height, I'd say, with a kind and gentle face. Warm smile. Great bedside manner, too. But he's kinda funny, y'know."

He waited for her to continue.

"You can't tell how old he is. One minute he looks pretty old, and then he looks younger. Mebbe it's the way the light plays on his face, or somethin'."

"Interesting. I'd better watch closely."

"But y'know, when he looks at you, he really *looks*. Like he's borin' right into your soul. Know what I mean?"

"I think so."

Just as the man followed the woman across the threshold into the waiting room, two men in dark suits shoved their way past him and marched directly into the back room where the doctor dispensed his treatments.

"Hey!"

"Get in line!"

"What you t'ink you doing?"

"Wait your turn."

The howls from the outraged petitioners bounced off the offenders like ping-pong balls from a hot stove. Closing the door behind them, the rude intruders confronted a gray-haired man in a rumpled gray sweater who seemed to be holding a bleeding gash on the arm of a scruffy-haired boy.

"Are you the doctor?" The voice was gruff.

"No," the man replied, continuing his ministrations without looking up.

"Well, what do you call what you're doing?"

"I'm healing this cut."

"And you say you're not a doctor?"

"That's right."

"*Sure.* You're just masquerading as a doctor. You're under arrest. You'll have to come with us."

"Just as soon as I finish what I'm doing." He continued ministering to the cut. "Ah ... would you mind explaining to the people waiting outside why they won't get any more healing today?"

The interlopers recognized the trap. "Never mind that. Just come with us. Now!" They handcuffed the healer and led him through the waiting room to a car idling at the door.

"They're arresting me for healing people," he called to the waiting throng.

The resulting bedlam rattled windows a block away. The waiting crowd surged toward the black car, rocking it to the verge of capsizing as it slinked away.

The man in the red-and-black striped tie entered the anteroom of the District Attorney's office, announcing himself to the secretary polishing her nails. She nodded him toward the inner office. Entering without a word, he placed a thin folder on the desk of Thomas "Slam Dunk" Slovny, Assistant District Attorney.

The ADA picked up the folder and glanced through the skimpy contents. "Not much here. How come?"

"Just as it was my turn to go in for treatment, your two goons shoved their way in and hauled him away. I stayed behind to look at his clinic but, except for a little furniture, it was pretty much an empty room."

"No medical equipment and things?"

"Not even a stethoscope."

"Damn."

"I talked to the woman in line in front of me. She said he could heal anything. It could be at least partly true, I suppose. The people coming out seemed pretty healthy and in high spirits."

"Well, we'll see about *that*."

The courtroom was packed with squirming, grumbling spectators, causing ADA Slovny to beam in anticipation. He scanned the seething crowd, savoring the thought of the delicious victory waiting just minutes away. *I'll show those snivelers how the law works around here. A dose of hard-assed justice is just what this case needs.* An election was coming up, and Mr. Slovny had his eye on the District Attorney's chair. *This is going to be a lead-pipe cinch. Imagine the defendant insisting on defending himself.*

"I won't need an attorney," the healer had told the judge during arraignment. "The facts will speak for themselves."

The veiled contempt oozing from that statement riled Mr. Slovny. *I'll slice that idiot into ribbons of raw flesh.* Especially galling was the defendant's refusal to give his name and home address to the booking officer. "Joe Healer," he insisted on calling himself when pressed.

We'll see about that, too, Slovny thought, drumming his fingers on the table.

The door to the judge's chambers opened and the judge entered the courtroom. After the preliminaries were completed and the charges read, Mr. Healer was directed to approach the bench. "It says here you've waived a jury trial. Is that correct?"

"Yes, Your Honor. And I still want to be my own defense counsel."

The judge frowned. "You do understand that a man who defends himself is said to have a fool for a client?" She continued frowning as she tried to pinpoint the man's age.

"Yes, Your Honor."

"All right, I'll allow it. But you've been warned. Now step back." The judge turned to the prosecutor. "As there is no jury for this case, you may call your first witness."

Thomas Slovny seemed to expand as he grinned and lifted himself from the creaking swivel chair. Taking his time to stroll from the prosecutor's table to the empty jury box, he waved an arm toward the defendant and began.

"Your Honor, this man is charged with practicing medicine without a license, and I intend to prove beyond a shadow of a doubt that this is *exactly* what he was doing when arrested and—"

"Get on with it," the judge interrupted. "This isn't a capital case, so you can forget your opening histrionics."

Undaunted, Slovny continued as though the judge hadn't spoken. "I call Dr. Charles A. Farquart to the stand."

A tall gray-haired man in a dark suit came forward and stood by the witness chair. After stating his name and occupation, he was sworn to tell the truth. He took his seat and folded his arms.

"Now then, Dr. Farquart, you are a doctor of medicine?"

"I believe that's why I've been summoned."

At the defense table, Mr. Healer steepled his fingers and rested his nose on their tips.

"And I believe you are currently the president of the American Medical Society?"

"That is correct." Dr. Farquart continued to enumerate the remainder of his qualifications.

"Now then, Doctor, this man is accused of practicing medicine without a license. I wonder if you would tell the court just how the practice of medicine is defined."

"I beg your pardon?"

"Just what *is* the practice of medicine? Surely a man of your medical stature can provide the court with a succinct definition of the practice of medicine?" Slovny began to regret not prepping his witness more thoroughly.

Recognizing the prosecutor was edging dangerously close to impeaching his own witness, the judge leaned forward, picked up a pen and scribbled a note.

"Uh … yes. Well … uh, I've never been asked for a definition before. The practice of medicine is pretty obvious, you know."

"I'd appreciate it if you'd define it for the court."

"All right. Well, medicine is any substance used in treating illnesses, and the practice of medicine is the art and science of medication— the dispensation and application of those medicines."

"Is that all?"

"No, of course not. It is the art and science of curing diseases with drugs and other curative procedures … including surgery."

"Thank you, Doctor. And what is involved in becoming qualified to practice medicine?"

"A medical degree, generally achieved after eight years of study." Almost as an afterthought, he added, "That, and passing the State Medical Board exam."

"Without which I presume no one is allowed to practice medicine in this state?"

"That is correct." He added, "And there is a penalty for doing so."

"Thank you, Doctor. You may be excused." The prosecutor turned to the spectators and beamed as though he'd just won the World Chess Tournament. "I call Mrs. Tanya Beloris to the stand."

"Just a moment," the judge interrupted. Turning to the defendant, she asked, "Do you have any questions for this witness, Mr. Healer?"

"Not at this time, Your Honor."

Mrs. Beloris, a spry woman of advancing years, waved to the gallery as she made her way to the stand. After being sworn, she sat erect in the witness chair and waggled her white gloves in the direction of familiar faces.

"Now then, Mrs. Beloris, I understand you've been treated by Mr. Healer there." He gestured toward the defendant.

"Oh, yes. Without his magic I'd be in the poorhouse by now."

"Could you explain that, please?"

"Sure. I'm a cleaning woman, you see, down at the LaProose building. If that nice man hadn't cured my back problem and my emphysema and everything, I wouldn't be able to work."

"He actually cured your emphysema?"

"Oh, yes. I used to be a smoker, you see. That made my lungs black and I had trouble catching my breath. Couldn't climb a flight of stairs without wheezing. The doctors I went to just shook their heads and said there wasn't much they could do. Then I heard about the Doc there—"

"Healer," the defendant corrected.

"Yeah ... healer. Whatever. He fixed me up good as new. Real wizard, he is."

"Thank you, Mrs. Beloris." Turning to the defendant, he said, "Your witness."

"No questions at this time," the defendant said, studying his fingernails.

The prosecutor frowned. The case was moving along much too quickly. At this pace, it would be over too soon for him to milk it of all its publicity value. As long as the defendant refused to ask questions, however, he had no choice but to continue.

One after another, the prosecutor called six more "patients," each of whom swore their ailments were cured by Mr. Healer. After dismissing the last witness—the defendant had no questions for any of them—Slovny turned to the jury box. Seeing it was empty, he turned his attention to the judge. *God, how I wish I could play to a jury. I can see the headlines now.*

"If the Court please, I believe I've proven that this man," he said, waving a dramatic arm in the direction of the defendant, "has treated dozens of people and apparently cured every one of them— regardless of the seriousness of their illness. It is obvious he is practicing medicine, and by his own admission he has no license permitting him to do so. Therefore, I urge the Court to find him guilty as charged and apply the fullest penalty allowed by the law." He spread his arms in triumph. "The prosecution rests its case."

"It's your turn, Mr. Healer," the judge said to the defendant. "Do you have a case to present?"

"Yes, Your Honor." Turning to the spectators, he called, "Mrs. Beloris. Would you please return to the stand?"

"Why, of course, Doctor, er, Mister Healer." She smiled and settled herself into the witness chair.

"Remember, you are still under oath. Mrs. Beloris, you testified that you came to see me on several occasions. Is that correct?"

"Yes."

"And why did you come to *me* instead of your family Doctor?"

"I *did* go to my family Doctor," she said, bristling. "Most of the time she just gave me prescriptions for expensive pills that made me feel worse."

"I see. And each time you came to me you went away satisfied?"

"And why not? No matter what my trouble was, you cured it right up. And you saved the life of my little boy, too."

"Now think about this carefully, Mrs. Beloris. Did I ever offer you any kind of medicine?"

"No-o-o, not that I remember."

"Did I ever ask you to take a pill or drink a liquid?"

"No, never."

"Did I ever stick you with a needle?"

She laughed. "No way. I'd remember that."

"Did I ever cut into your skin with a scalpel or any other kind of instrument?"

"Absolutely not!"

"Finally, Mrs. Beloris, did I ever charge you for my services?"

"Not one red cent! Well, I left a little donation in your basket when I was able, but you never asked for no money."

"Thank you, Mrs. Beloris. That will be all."

A troubled prosecutor jumped to his feet and shouted, "Wait just a minute, Mrs. Beloris. I have a few questions on re-direct."

"What's that mean?" she asked.

"It means I want to clear up an item or two. You say this Mr. Healer here never gave you medicine, or pills, or injections. Is that right?"

"Right as rain."

"But you went away cured?"

"Sure did."

"Then what, may I ask what, *did* he do?"

The defendant smiled behind his steepled fingers. The prosecutor had walked right into his trap and was about to help prove his case.

Mrs. Beloris had to think about the question she'd been asked. "It's kinda hard to say. When I fell down the stairs and broke my wrist he held my wrist with the tips of his fingers."

"Is that all?"

"Well, he moved it around a little—gentle like—and it got pretty hot, but before I knew what was happening, it stopped hurting. And when I hacked my way into his office with the emphysema he just sat in front of me. Then he held my hands and stared at me with those nice black eyes of his."

"That's *all*?" The prosecutor began to see his "slam-dunk" case slipping away. So sure the case would require only half his brain, he was now sorry he had skimped on preparation. Looking for a lifeline, he stared directly at his star witness.

Dr. Farquart ignored the pleading look and shrugged.

"Surely he gave you some medicine, or a shot?"

"No. Never. Well … during my emphysema visit he put one hand on my chest and one on my back at the same time. Felt warm and fuzzy, it did." Then, in a lame attempt to help the poor prosecutor man, she added, "Maybe he cures people by smothering them with kindness."

The courtroom erupted with laughter and the judge banged her gavel for silence.

"Your *Honor*," whined the prosecutor.

"Sorry," replied the judge, barely suppressing the guffaw welling up inside her. "You stepped into that one all by yourself. Now move along, please."

He waved a hand of dismissal at his witness. "That will be all, Mrs. Beloris. Thank you very much." She stepped down and curtsied as the audience applauded.

The defendant called the other five witnesses in turn, repeating the questions he'd asked of Mrs. Beloris, each time receiving the same answers. No, he hadn't given them any medicines or potions, hadn't stuck them with a needle or cut into their bodies. What's more, he hadn't asked for payment.

His approach to the last witness, however, was somewhat different. Mr. Sarsonal, a bricklayer for a local contractor, gave the same answers to the key questions. When he began to rise from the witness chair, however, his exit was interrupted.

"One moment, Mr. Sarsonal. I have just a few more questions."

The witness settled back into the chair.

"Mr. Sarsonal, I believe you told me your wife is diabetic."

"That's right. I tried to get her to go to *you*, but she didn't want to piss off her regular doctor."

"I understand. What kind of treatment does your wife get from her doctor?"

"He gives her shots to take at home."

"She gives herself those shots—for the diabetes?"

"No, I do it for her. She doesn't like needles, y'see, so it's easier on her if I do it. That way she doesn't have to look."

"I see. So if I understand you correctly, you prepare the shot using the medication the doctor prescribed?"

"Yeah. That's right."

"And then you insert the needle into your wife's skin?"

"Sure. Nothing to it … well, I try to get her to laugh a little before I stick her."

The defendant paused before continuing. "Mr. Sarsonal, have *you* ever been arrested for practicing medicine without a license?"

There was a moment of total silence in the stunned courtroom, followed by a rising crescendo of murmurs as the bombshell penetrated the consciousness of the spectators.

The prosecutor leaped to his feet and waved his arms. "Now just a minute here—"

"Unless you've got some sort of objection," the judge said, "move back and sit down."

"But the defense is impeaching his own witness."

"Which he has a perfect right to do. Now sit *down*."

The ADA scowled his way back to his seat.

Mr. Healer turned back to the witness. "Mr. Sarsonal, do you have a medical degree?"

"Of course not! I'm just giving my wife the shots and pills the doctor told me to give her. What do I need with a medical degree? Ain't nothin' to it."

"And your doctor understands that you medicate your wife with the shots he prescribes?"

"Of course he does!"

"I ask you again, Mr. Sarsonal, *have* you ever been arrested for practicing medicine without a license?"

Sarsonal leaped to his feet and leaned toward the questioner. "Of course not, you idiot! What kind of fool question is that?"

"Thank you, Mr. Sarsonal. You may step down."

The judge banged her gavel to quell the hubbub ballooning in the courtroom.

"Your Honor," Mr. Healer began, "I believe the prosecutor has correctly convinced the Court that the legal definition of the 'practice of medicine' involves both dispensing and applying medications, as well as the art of surgery. He has also shown that to practice medicine in accordance with its legal definition, a license from the State is required. I have just demonstrated that Mr. Sarsonal, who admits he does *not* have a medical degree, dispenses medication to his wife by means of injections and pills—injections and pills prescribed by their own family doctor. Therefore, your Honor, I believe Mr. Sarsonal is guilty of practicing medicine without a license and should be arrested for that offense ... as should every other citizen behaving in a similar manner."

The uproar was deafening. The judge's pounding gavel did little to abate the shouting and hooting.

The prosecutor leaped to his feet and shouted, "Objection! Objection!" His complaint was lost in the wall of angry voices.

When, at long last, order was restored, the judge spoke, the glint in her eye unmistakable. "You've made your point, Mr. Healer. The law does indeed require a medical degree and a license for anyone wishing to practice medicine."

"Thank you, Your Honor," Mr. Healer said, bowing slightly. "The law does *not*, however, equate the practice of *healing* with the practice of *medicine*. In other words, it is not illegal to heal if that healing is performed *outside* the constraints of medical laws."

"Could you expand on that, Mr. Healer?" the judge asked, a smile crinkling the skin around her eyes.

The healer nodded slightly and continued. "Thank you, Your Honor. The prosecutor seems to be operating from the assumption that healing is accomplished solely through the practice of medicine. But that assumption is false. Though the goal of the medical profession is to heal, the practice of medicine is not the *only* source of healing. It is not a reversible equation. All medical practitioners attempt to heal, but not all healing is accomplished by medical practitioners."

"Can you provide the Court with an example?"

"Yes, your Honor. All musicians attempt to entertain, but not all entertainment is provided by musicians. All plumbers repair leaky pipes, but not all leaky pipes are repaired by plumbers. All medical practitioners attempt to heal, but not all healing is provided by medical practitioners. Healing is often effected by parents, psychologists, the clergy, and by friends skilled in the art of listening, to name just a few. Shall I go on?"

The judge held up a hand. "That will do, sir. Let's see where we stand. I believe the prosecutor has demonstrated that healing through the practice of medicine requires a license—in the absence of which one is committing illegal acts. On that we all agree, I believe."

The prosecutor turned to the gallery and beamed.

"But through his cross-examination of your … er … patient, the prosecutor has *also* demonstrated that you are a successful healer. And though I'm sure he didn't mean to do so, he clearly established that you accomplish your healing through means *other* than those falling within the definition of medical practice. Without, in other words, breaking the law. I therefore rule in favor of the defense. Mr. Healer, you are free to go—and return to your good works. Case dismissed."

The erupting applause was robust, and the catcalls directed at the prosecutor bordered on the obscene.

The prosecutor's body seemed to shrivel as he returned to his seat. He leaned his elbows on the table, dropped his head onto his hands, and sighed.

Just as the judge began to rise, the healer raised his hand. "May I have a moment, please."

"Of course," she said, frowning.

"Thank you for the judgment in my favor, Your Honor, but I do not intend to continue my work. At least, not here."

"May I ask why not?" As she spoke, the judge noticed the man seemed considerably older than when the trial began.

"Your Honor, I have discovered that, on this planet, the desire to heal bodies and spirits is overshadowed by the desire to use the infirmities of others as a vehicle for achieving fame and fortune."

"I beg your pardon?" The judge seemed perplexed.

"For example, medicines that don't work are allowed to be advertised by the drug companies. *Effective* treatments are often shunned—outlawed even—by government agencies, if they cannot be made profitable by the drug cartel. Thousands of wasteful surgical procedures are carried out, adding unnecessary financial burdens for patients and their families. These are condoned, even though they cause thousands upon thousands of *avoidable* deaths each and every year.

"Add to that the cost of the thousands of medical errors committed every year, and the cost and inconvenience caused by the diseases patients acquire *during* their hospital stays. The enormity of this unnecessary waste of lives and money boggles the mind.

"In this climate, your Honor, my own spirit shrivels, and my life force ebbs in despair. I must move on or die where I stand."

On those words, he raised his hands above his head and touched his fingers together. Electricity crackled and the air shimmered. Then, as the spectators gasped, he simply dissolved and vanished, leaving nothing behind but a wisp of smoke and the smell of ozone in the air.

BALLET LOVE

▼

Tanyika snuggled against her lover's bare chest and sighed. "You danced very well tonight, Ivan. The audience loved you." She lifted her head to look into his dark eyes.

"And you looked good enough to eat, flitting about in that hummingbird costume," Ivan said. He removed the silver comb from her black hair and combed it down around her bare shoulders.

"Why do you always call this my hummingbird costume? I'm supposed to be a nymph."

"Because that's what it reminds me of." He tousled her lacy ruffles. "But how do you know how well I danced? Weren't you too busy keeping pace with the other ballerinas to notice?"

She poked him in his well-defined ribs with a knuckle. "Don't be so modest. You know your leaps brought generous applause."

"I'll admit I felt pretty good tonight. But that's because I kept looking in your direction. I kept wanting to hold you in my arms—like this." He stroked her bare back and held her tight. "Will you have a late dinner with me tonight?"

"Not tonight. I must work on my pirouettes. You know I want to be a prima ballerina one day, and the only way I can do that is by working even harder." She took one of his hands and playfully bit a finger. "I'm glad you care, Ivan, but if we don't begin to attract larger audiences, Mr. Weinkopf will have to close us down."

Saul Weinkopf, Managing Director of the ballet troupe, sat in his disheveled office nursing a cigar stub and brushing ashes from his once-white shirt. He was thinking about that very problem. The anemic week's receipts spread on the desk in front of him didn't make him happy, and he scowled at his visitor to convey his displeasure. He waved his hands over the rumpled receipts. "Well, what do you have to say for yourself, Sergei? Are you planning to lead us into bankruptcy within the month?"

Sergei Vanovich, ballet master and choreographer, sat stiffly in the chair opposite, twirling his black silver-topped cane between his legs. "Me? Why is it *my* fault? I drive them as hard as I can, and even your lead dancers, Olga and Roberto, are improving. But there's only so much blood I can squeeze from those onions. You want to know why sales stink? Go look at your so-called marketing program, and the sleazy venues you book."

"Now look here, you over-inflated peacock, I've had about enough of your bloated ego. Keep that up and I'll break your other leg and toss you into the nearest dumpster."

Sergei tossed his head and harrumphed. "After which you will do *what* for a living?" Leaning over the desk to stare at Saul's ballooning belly, he sneered. "Ah. Perhaps they will hire you at the circus and advertise you as 'The Human Blimp'."

Saul raised his hands in submission and sighed. "Okay, Okay, enough play-time. We got a serious problem here. What are we gonna do about it?"

A loud knock interrupted Sergei's response.

"Yeah?"

The door opened and a tall, muscular man entered. He ran a hand through his thick hair and said, "I'm told I should talk to a Mr. Saul Weinkopf—"

"Yeah. That's me. What can I do for you?"

Sergei took that as his cue to leave. Rising, he waved to Saul and closed the door behind him.

"My name is Rodenski and I've come to audition for the role of premier danseur."

"Excuse me, Mr. Rodenski, but *here* you audition for a job as dancer. *We* decide who become the stars."

"I understand, sir. However, I believe you will find it to your immense advantage if you allow me to audition. Then you can decide what to do with me."

"Fair enough."

"There is one condition."

"A condition? You're asking for a job—for premier danseur, no less—and you got conditions? I know lots of arrogant dancers, Rodenski, but this brings new meaning to the word 'chutzpah'."

"Please hear me out. I'm asking to dance for you in secret so you alone will know what I can do. That way, you can use that knowledge in your own best interests."

Saul had never been in this situation before. Though put off by the man's arrogance, his curiosity was aroused. "What can you possibly do that needs to be seen in secret?"

"If you will indulge me, sir, I guarantee you will not waste your time."

Saul twirled a pencil. "Oh, okay. There's a practice studio down the hall."

"Begging your pardon, Mr. Weinkopf. Would it be possible to use the stage?"

"The stage? What's wrong with the studio?"

"The ceiling isn't high enough. Please, let me dance on the stage—with the doors locked."

"You got a lotta nerve, buddy. I just hope you got something to back it up." He rose as he spoke and led the dancer toward the stage. It was nearly midnight and the theater looked deserted. Even so, Saul locked the doors and hollered, "Anybody here?" There being no response, he turned to Rodenski and asked, "You need music?"

"No. And the stage light will be just fine. Just sit in the audience and watch."

Saul squeezed his bulk into a third-row seat and fondled an unlit cigar.

Tanyika and Ivan dreamed as they lingered over the remainder of their white Chablis.

"I'm glad you decided to have dinner with me tonight, Tanny."

"I really shouldn't have. I should be practicing."

"I know. But I love being with you, and we can always work harder tomorrow. Our dream will come true, Tanny. Just imagine. The two of us ... you the prima ballerina and me the premier danseur. We will have glorious times."

The other diners had long gone and the lone waiter hovered by the bar. He didn't mind. He could see love in the eyes of his young customers, and that made him smile. Thinking of his own first romance, he wondered if they were lovers. As if pleased with his logic, he mumbled, "No, if they were lovers, they'd have headed for her apartment hours ago. But they just sit there talking and holding hands. It won't be long, though."

"Come in, Tanyika, and sit down, please."

"Your message said I should come as soon as possible. Is something wrong, Mr. Weinkopf?"

"No, no. Not at all." He gestured to the tall man beside him. "This is Rodenski, our new premier danseur. He has something to ask you."

Tanyika sucked in her breath at the news. "New? I don't understand. What about—?"

Rodenski was about to speak when Weinkopf interrupted. "I'll explain about them in a minute. Tanyika, something wonderfully special has come up." He motioned to Rodenski to continue the explanation.

Rodenski said, "Mr. Weinkopf has graciously allowed me to select a partner for our performance Saturday evening." He took her hand in his. "I am hoping you will accept my offer to be my prima ballerina."

Tanyika stepped back and put a hand over her mouth, eyes wide with surprise. "I ... I don't know what to say." Her mind racing with images of applause and glory, she glanced at Weinkopf. "Is this some sort of prank at my expense?"

"Not at all. Mr. Weinkopf has explained that you are a very good dancer, and everyone can see you are young and beautiful." *You also don't weigh much.*

Tanyika's breathing became more rapid as she absorbed the startling offer. *What will Ivan say when he hears the news? I've never been faced with such a difficult decision—either accept the offer as lead dancer with a man I've never seen dance, and lose my beloved, or refuse the incredible offer and ...*

Weinkopf snapped her tortured reverie with unexpected tenderness. "You are perhaps wondering how your boyfriend will take the news, no? I can't say, but if he is the man you believe him to be, he will glory in your opportunity."

She stared hard at Rodenski.

"Come," he said, smiling. "It will be grand. We will work hard together, and you will captivate the audience. Please dance with me."

"I ... I don't think I'm ready for—"

"Even if that were true," Rodenski interrupted, "it wouldn't matter. I will guarantee that you will dance magnificently."

Bowing her head, she said, "All right. I will do my very best."

"You will not be pleased at my news," Tanyika said to Ivan when they met in the rehearsal hall the following morning.

"But how could my lovely lady possibly displease me?"

"You will see." She tugged him to the stools in a corner of the room and motioned him to sit. Sitting beside him with eyes lowered, she described the incredible event of the night before. Both happy and sad at the same time, her words tumbled out like a blanket of blossoms floating on a rock-strewn stream.

Ivan was stunned. His face darkened and a tear formed.

"I am sorry," she whispered. "Truly, I am, but I could not bring myself to turn down such a wonderful opportunity." Her own eyes misted over as well.

"Look at you," Ivan said, lifting her chin with a gentle hand. "You shed tears, but your eyes gleam with excitement at the same time. How could I not be pleased with your good fortune?"

"Then we will still be friends?"

"Of course. My love for you deepens as we speak." But his words barely hid his disappointment as his mind formed pictures of the days to come. *The spotlights and the applause will beguile my beloved and turn her head from me.* His hands balled into fists as he fantasized scenes of catastrophe. *We will no longer dance as equals, and I will lose her to this intruding stranger. Without her beside me, I will be nothing but an unhappy nobody.*

Tanyika could feel the sadness behind his expression of love. "I am truly sorry if this hurts you. I hoped you would be glad for me. Please try, Ivan." She picked up her dancing shoes and added, "Now I must go. There is much for me to learn before the performance."

Ivan balled his fists in anger as he stepped from the theatre into a moonless night. *Who is this dancing Svengali who steals my love?*

Weinkopf's spirits soared as he bustled to prepare for Saturday's performance. While watching Rodenski's audition dance, his skin crawled and his eyes widened at the dancer's every move. He could not believe what he was seeing. His mind was electrified by the possibilities and he now worked to turn them into reality. He raced from office to office, barking orders for a new set for the second act, for more and bigger advertisements, for new programs, for a telephone campaign to patrons, present and past. He had much to do.

He thought about this morning's meeting with his backers. When they learned of the lavish expenditure of funds in support of a lackluster ballet, they expressed a unanimous opinion.

"Have you gone *mad*?" they chorused.

But Saul Weinkopf would not reveal his secret, even to them. "Just wait," he smirked. "You'll see. And if you don't bring all your friends, they will hate you for not allowing them to experience this miraculous event."

After the grumbling backers left, he dragged the stage manager onto the noisy sidewalk. "I don't want anyone to overhear our conversation. Saturday will be very special, and the rehearsals for the next three days must be held in strict secrecy. I will hold you responsible for making sure no one—do you hear me?—*no one* other than Tanyika and Rodenski will get *close* to the stage during their rehearsals. Is that clear?" He emphasized his point by stabbing the air with a frayed cigar.

"I don't understand—and what about musicians?"

"You don't *need* to understand, and musicians won't be required. But it is critical that you keep the secret to yourself until the performance. Everyone's job may depend on it—especially yours. Can I count on you?"

The sun appeared the following morning for the first time in five days of cloudy gloom, brightening Weinkopf's spirits, still bubbling from the evening before. When Rodenski arrived minutes later, Saul led him to the practice studio where the day's rehearsal was already under way.

As soon as he and the stranger entered, the change in Weinkopf's demeanor was instantly noticed. His grinning ebullience aroused speculation by everyone in the troupe, eager to learn the cause of this sudden transformation.

"I have something to tell you," Weinkopf began, letting his eyes slowly roam the room. Assured that no one other than the cast was present, he motioned the dancers to gather around him. "I have an announcement of momentous importance, and you must promise not to breathe a word I tell you until our secret is revealed Saturday night. His eyes scanned the dancers until he detected a nod of agreement from each. "I guarantee that the rewards for your cooperation will be great."

Weinkopf's introduction of Rodenski was greeted by a buzz of puzzled conversation. Holding up his hands for silence, he shouted, "Hold it down, hold it down. We all need to work together to make this work." When he explained that Rodenski and Tanyika would be taking over as lead dancers for the second act, the muttering turned into shouts of defiance.

"What about Olga and Roberto?"

"Yeah. We already got lead dancers."

"Good ones, too. Why are you doing this to us?"

Besieged with hostile questions, Weinkopf strolled to Olga and Roberto and put an arm around each. "These wonderful dancers know the whole story, and they agree it is a good plan. Besides, we will open the performance as usual. Rodenski and Tanyika will only dance the last act."

Olga and Roberto nodded. "Listen to Mr. Weinkopf," Roberto said. "This *will* be a good thing for all of us. Like he said, Olga and I are behind the plan one hundred percent."

Mollified, the troupe allowed the Managing Director to continue. "What you need to know is that all of you will continue rehearsals as though nothing unusual is happening. Rodenski and Tanyika will rehearse on the stage, and will dance the second—last—act at the performance. Other than that, I can tell you that all the seats have already been sold and the house will be standing room only."

"I don't like this Rodenski person. I've never even heard of him," Ivan groused as he and Tanny headed for the deli across the street. "He seems so smug. You've rehearsed with him a whole day now. Can he dance?"

Tanyika burned to tell him the secret of their rehearsals, but dared not. A leak would spoil everything. "Yes, he can dance, and this will be a wonderful opportunity for me—and for everyone else."

Though her partner tried to worm the secret from her, she remained steadfast. The cost of doing otherwise was too great.

On Saturday night, Weinkopf could not restrain himself from peeking through the curtain again and again to revel at the packed house. Every seat was already filled, and the standing room at the rear of the theatre was jammed. He scanned faces in the loges for his backers. He sensed they were not yet convinced that he had spoken the truth, but was sure they must be impressed by the size of the audience. He peeked through the curtain yet again.

The buzz of conversation grew louder as the audience waited, stimulated by the discovery of unfamiliar names in their program.

"Who is this Rodenski? I've never heard of him."

"What happened to Olga and Roberto?

"Why aren't they dancing the entire ballet?"

"Were they fired? Are they ill?

"This isn't the way it's done."

Speculation sloshed from one end of the hall and back again.

Backstage, Rodenski motioned the troupe to gather around him. "Tanyika and I want to thank you for your cooperation these past three days. I realize it has been hard work, but you will be well rewarded for your efforts ... and for your discretion." Then he told them about what they would see after his entrance during the second act.

The dancers' shaking heads made it clear they didn't believe what they just heard. They looked at Tanyika, who smiled and nodded her confirmation.

After the gasps subsided, Rodenski added, "You will heighten the effect by pretending nothing special is happening. Just continue dancing in your usual competent manner."

He then took Tanyika aside and said, "Now remember, as long as you hold onto my hand, nothing can happen to you. As you have seen during our rehearsals, you have nothing to fear. You dance beautifully, and I am proud to have you as my partner."

When the orchestra finished tuning, the lights dimmed and the conductor entered, dipping his head in response to the customary applause. As he raised his baton, the overture began.

When the curtains opened during the final cadence and the stage lights brightened, the audience gasped with delight at the sight of the new set. The stage had been transformed to depict the holiday atmosphere of a village festival already in progress. Colorful lanterns hung from swaying wires, streamers dangled from trees, and each "villager" wore a bright costume representing a favorite fantasy.

The ballet told the story of a pair of young peasants, danced by Olga and Roberto, who meet at a village festival. While watching the dance contest, during which each villager performs a solo dance as revelers sing and clap, the two young peasants have eyes only for each other. When it is the young woman's turn to begin her dance, she points to her chosen one and beckons for the love-struck young man to join her. They are so carried away by their love, they win the contest.

Once the dance contest ends, the revelry continues until the carousers wear themselves out and leave the stage. As the curtain closes the first act, Olga and Roberto fall asleep in each others' arms under an upstage tree.

The burst of applause that followed, accompanied by smiles and laughter, stamped the performance an immediate success. The exuberant ovation could be heard by the performers in their dressing rooms a floor below.

"They like it, don't they?" Ivan said to Tanyika. "I haven't heard this much applause since joining the troupe. Now it will be your turn to blow them out of their chairs." He kissed her lightly on the forehead.

"Oh, Ivan, I do so wish you were dancing with me."

"I do, too, my sweet. But that would ruin the entire surprise, wouldn't it?"

Five minutes before the intermission ended, all the patrons had returned to their seats. Though such promptness was most unusual, everyone burned with curiosity to see what this Rodenski person was all about.

The lights dimmed ten minutes later and the conductor's baton slashed the air to begin the second act overture. When it ended, he paused.

The lengthening silence raised the tension almost more than the audience could bear.

As the fidgeting and murmuring began to spread, the curtains opened and the stage lights illuminated an unexpected sight. Brightly-colored silk banners hung across the back of the stage, shimmering and sparkling from the very top of the proscenium to the floor below. Eight living trees were "planted" on mounds covered in living grass, and growing flowers added to the illusion of a peaceful forest glade. On a grassy knoll far upstage, the young peasant lovers—Olga and Roberto—continued to dream their fantasies.

When the applause faded way, kettledrums roared to a crescendo, capped by the crashing of three large cymbals. The silk banners came alive, billowing in response to every movement of the nymphs dancing across the stage.

Then, as trumpets blared, Rodenski leaped onto the stage. He wore a black shimmering fabric that appeared molded to his body, the material sparkling with every movement of his arms and legs.

He began his solo with one continuous twirl that took him the full width of the stage, the constant movement of the white silk scarf fastened to his left wrist adding excitement to every turn and dip.

The audience gasped at this astonishing feat.

Pausing to regain his breath, Rodenski looked up at the invisible sky and stretched out his left arm as if to point to the stars. Then he leaped. Up, and up, and up, half way to the proscenium forty feet in the air. Moving in a perfect arc, he gently returned to the other edge of the stage and kneeled before Tanyika, costumed as the Queen of the nymphs.

The audience sprang to its feet as one, electrified by what they had just seen, reluctant to believe their eyes. When their initial awe subsided, spontaneous applause filled the theatre. The noise was so deafening it completely masked their comments of incredulity.

"Did you see that?'

"How did he do that?"

"Is he attached to a wire?"

"It's impossible to leap like that."

"It must be an optical illusion."

During the explosion of emotion and wonder, the dancers on stage remained frozen in position, as did the musicians who waited for the cue to continue. It was a long time coming.

When the audience finally settled into their seats, their eyes remained glued to the two dancers.

When the music resumed, Rodenski said, "Now remember, Tanyika, as long as you hold my hand, you cannot fall. Now come ... let us dance." His raised hand beckoned her to join him.

Rising to his feet, he guided her through the first bars of their dance. Their movements were delicate, eloquent, and precise. But there were no astonishing leaps and the audience began to wonder if they had actually seen what they thought they had.

At last, Rodenski and Tanyika entered the well-known courting scene during which all the dancers of the troupe circled the two leads standing center-stage. On cue from the booming kettledrums and trilling flutes, they faced one another. Tanyika placed her hands into those of her partner, and they began to twirl. Slowly at first, then faster and faster. When it seemed impossible for them to move any faster, they lifted slowly from the stage and twirled their way toward the stars, the silk banners behind them billowing in response to the dancers' energetic movement.

The audience again leapt to their feet with mouths agape. Was this a miracle? A trick? An illusion? Some applauded while others simply stood in place, stunned, their hearts pounding.

Having been carefully briefed, the dancers below continued their performances as though nothing unusual were happening above them.

Ivan danced his part well, but found it more and more difficult to focus. His love was flying high above him, making it almost impossible to keep his eyes on the dancers around him. Even so, he had reasons to concentrate. The troupe danced as never before and he wanted to be part of their shining performance. More urgently, he wanted to look good in Tanny's eyes.

Still high above the stage, Rodenski began swinging Tanyika around his head as though waving a large banner.

The effect on Tanyika was intoxicating. Not only had her dream come true, not only was she the prima ballerina on whom everyone's eyes were riveted, she was dancing in mid-air with a man whose touch was absolute magic. She felt she could fly like this forever. *This is beyond wonderful. I feel so light and free, I could ...*

Tanyika's fantasy so overpowered her concentration that she let her hands slip from Rodenski's and began falling toward the stage far below. She drifted downward slowly at first, and then, as Rodenski's residual energy dissipated, faster and faster.

Yet again the audience gasped, this time in horror. As if pulled by a string, they leaned forward in unison and grasped the seatbacks in front of them, certain they were about to see a tragic accident.

Tanyiki fell with panic on her face. Too frightened to scream, she flailed her arms and kicked her feet, looking like anything but the graceful dancer of only a few moments before. Down and down she plunged. As the stage rushed toward her, she could think only, *"I'm going to die!"*

As soon as Rodenski felt her hands slipping from his, he knew what he must do. There was no time for grace or elegance; it was a time for instant action. Arms outstretched, he swooped toward the stage, hoping he would be in time.

Then, just as Tanyika drew her last breath, he reached out, caught her in his arms, and floated her gently to the stage.

White with terror, Tanyika muttered, *"Oh God, oh God!"* Wiping the tears streaming down her cheeks, she stuttered, "I'm ... I'm so ... so sorry." She couldn't believe she was still alive. Her body stiff with panic, her whitened fingers clung to her rescuer's shoulders. She turned her head from the audience to hide her humiliation.

"Stop it," Rodenski shouted at her over the wild ovation, pinching various parts of her anatomy to attract attention from her fright. "You are not hurt. The audience thinks it was all part of the dance. You can panic later, but for now, pull yourself together and smile." He pried her hands loose from around his body and pulled her to her feet.

She managed a limp smile, and together they bowed to one another, signaling the music to continue for the final minutes of the ballet.

When the last chord sounded and the curtains closed, the audience slumped exhausted in their seats. Silence filled the hall as everyone paused to regain their calm after the emotional roller-coaster just experienced.

A few moments later, the curtains parted for the curtain calls. Pandemonium erupted. Once again the audience rose to its feet, whistling, shouting, and applauding as each performer in turn stepped forward to bow.

"Brava!"

"Bravo!"

When it was Rodenski's and Tanyiki's turn to bow, the applause and shouting swelled to new heights.

Rodenski motioned for Olga and Roberto to join hands with them at center stage. When the four stepped forward for yet another bow, Rodenski lifted them a few feet from the stage to acknowledge the generous ovation.

The curtains closed for the last time after seventeen curtain calls. The tired, but energized, troupe couldn't stop hugging and kissing one another in jubilation. They crowded around Tanyika to express their awe and admiration at her execution of "the fall." They, too, thought it was part of the act, as Rodenski had briefed his partner not to broadcast the unrehearsed nature of that terrifying event.

Ivan joined in the post-performance celebration, but could only pretend to be pleased. *Tanny has found a new and wonderful life with Rodenski, and I will continue to be an invisible dancer for the rest of my life.* The more he thought about his imagined fate, the more depressed he became. Unable to share the joy a moment longer, he picked up his tote bag and slipped through the stage door into the darkened alley.

"Listen up, please!" Weinkopf had joined the spontaneous celebration in the Green Room under the stage. Waving his arms for attention, he continued, "Please, everyone, I have an announcement."

The word "announcement" was greeted with playful boos, after which they quieted enough for Weinkopf to continue.

"I don't need to tell you how marvelous you were tonight, and I don't have to tell you the audience loved what they saw. But I do have to tell you that even before the performance ended we began receiving offers from all around the world for our performances."

"Yeah? Like where? Bayonne?" a voice shouted.

"Everywhere. London, Rome, Tokyo, Moscow. You name it, and I probably have a telegram already in my hand." He waved a fistful of paper, beaming at the thought of managing a sellout show for years to come. His grin widened even further when he saw his backers snaking their way backstage to pay homage and hand him expensive cigars.

The cast party lasted until dawn.

The following months found Tanyika in a whirlwind of activity. Travel and performances in exotic parts of the world—new admirers to meet—fan mail to answer—non-stop radio, television, and newspaper interviews to endure. At first, the interviews were awkward because she wasn't sure how to respond to personal and intrusive questions. As she grew in confidence, however, she learned to charm even the most brutish reporters. When they demanded to know whether her "fall" was an accident or part of the act, she smiled coyly and said, "If I told you, you might not look forward to seeing it again."

"The fall" was a touchy subject. Having realized the publicity value of the breath-taking event, Rodenski implored Tanyika to let him keep it in their dance for every performance.

Tanyika refused. "No. Though you saved my life, I nearly died that night ... I couldn't stand to experience that terror again. You saw it yourself. My heart stopped and I was white with fear. I refuse to feel that way ever again."

"But—"

"No! We should be content with what we have," she repeated. "We fly for them every night and that should be enough."

Ivan also shared in the fame and growing wealth of his colleagues, more than he ever dreamed possible. Like the others, he, too, was besieged with requests for interviews, photos, and autographs. Like the others, he traveled to exotic locations and lived in comfortable accommodations. Like the others, his dancing added precision, flair, and sparkle. But he was not content. Every night he looked up to see his beloved in Rodenski's arms, swirling and swooping to the music, and every night he felt pain in his heart. *Yes, I have more than I ever dreamed of having, except for my true love. It is like having everything—and nothing. She is a star and has no time for a nobody like me.*

Every night, he drank in the applause and admiration of the enraptured audiences, yet his life was empty. Convinced that no amount of practice or improvement would bring her back to him, his heart began whispering that life was no longer worth living.

When the tour at last ended, the troupe returned to New York, totally exhausted, for a much-deserved rest. Though they bubbled with delight as they told and retold their adventures to all who would listen, they were numb with fatigue from the performing, packing, traveling, unpacking, and performing yet again.

This is the perfect time for me to resign and face my destiny, Ivan thought, standing outside Weinkopf's office door. As he reached for the knob, he heard voices from behind the frosted-glass window.

"This is impossible!" he heard Weinkopf shout. "You can't *do* this to me. This is treason! I've given you everything you asked for. I'll be *ruined*."

When Winkoph's fury abated, Ivan heard Rodenski's voice.

"No, you will not be ruined. Have you not seen the improvement in the dancers? They are now world class and will continue to acquit themselves accordingly. But I must leave."

"*Why* must you leave?" Weinkopf, feet wide-spread and fists planted on hips, jutted a belligerent chin toward the source of his imagined downfall and impending poverty. "Tell me why? What have I denied you?"

"You haven't denied me anything. But this is not about you. It is about me, and about what I must do. I have helped save your troupe and have filled your bags with money. But now I am called away. You have excellent dancers who will carry on." As he turned to leave, he added, "You could at least try to express a modicum of gratitude for what you have received."

Ivan flattened his trim body behind the door as Rodenski left, eager to tell Tanny what he had overheard. Once Rodenski was out of sight, he sprinted toward the studios where he was certain Tanny would be practicing. But she was not there. After looking everywhere, he finally found her sitting under a prop tree on the stage. Though her face was hidden in her hands, he could tell she was crying. His heart melted. *She must already know about that bastard Rodenski's traitorous plan.* He sat beside her and placed a gentle arm around her shoulders.

"Are you crying because you know of Rodenski plans to leave us?"

Between sobs, she nodded. "A few minutes ago he came to me and told me he would have to leave."

"Did he tell you why?"

"No. He said he would tell me as soon as he finished his talk with Weinkopf. I'm to wait for him here. Oh, Ivan. *Why* must it end? We've had such a marvelous time."

"Yes, dear one, we have. But you are a wonderful person, and stronger than you realize. Life will go on. You'll see."

She squeezed his hands, but no words came.

Pausing to gather his courage, Ivan at last dared to say what was in his heart. "I know I can't fly like Rodenski, but do you think we might be together again?"

Tanny's head snapped up as her eyes widened. "*Again?* But we have never been apart. My heart has *always* been yours."

Overjoyed by her words, Ivan wrapped his arms tightly around her and smothered her with kisses.

Between the blizzard of kisses, Tanyika said, "I know I've been blinded by fame, and I know I've neglected you during these busy, whirlwind months. But I thought of you every day and longed for your tender embraces, your touch—"

"Aha, I see you are already here," Rodenski said, striding across the stage toward the lovers. "I hope I'm not interrupting anything." Directing his next words to Ivan, he said, "I must speak in private with Tanyika. It will not take long. Do you mind?"

Of course I mind, you insensitive oaf! Ivan thought, conveying the message with a dour expression. "No, of course not," he lied. "I'll wait in the studio," striding from the stage.

"I'm sorry to interrupt what I sense was a tender moment," Rodenski said, settling next to Tanyika, "but I have something I must tell you."

"What more can you have to say after you told me you are abandoning the troupe?" The bitterness in her voice sliced through her words.

"Yes, it is true that it is time for me to leave, but please believe me when I say it is unavoidable." After a pause, he said, "I am not abandoning the troupe, my dear, nor am I leaving of my own desire. I am leaving because ... because I must die soon, and I want that final act to occur at a time and place of my own choosing. And I choose today. Here ... now."

Tanyika jumped up. "No! no! You must not die. *Please* don't die." She realized she was speaking foolish words, but the unexpected announcement scrambled her ability to think.

"Hear me out. When you asked me why I didn't teach others how to fly, I said I could not. That was the truth."

"I don't understand."

"Though I cannot teach others to fly, I can transfer the gift to one person—as it was transferred to me. When I do, my life force will be expended, and I will die." Taking her hands in his, he continued, "Tanyika, if you can bring yourself to accept the terms, I want *you* to receive this gift."

"Me? I ... I don't know what to say."

"Just say you will grant my last wish—after which you may have your own choice of partners. Please?"

"But ... but I will be responsible for your death—"

"No. I will expire within a few weeks no matter what I do today."

"I still don't understand."

"The gift burns the body's resources, aging it faster than does a life of normal activity. When that energy is expended, the body will die."

"How ... how long would *I* have to live?" Tanyika wanted to run away without hearing the answer, but she could not.

"It is now almost three years since I received the gift—but I am considerably older than you. With your younger and more resilient body, who can say?"

"Is there no other way?"

Rodenski shook his head. "I know of none. But if you accept the gift, you will earn much more than fame and fortune. You will be given a powerful opportunity to lift many hearts and spirits. You will know when it is over in time to pass the gift to someone else."

She looked into his eyes and knew he spoke the truth. "Let me see if I understand what you are saying. If I accept this gift, I will live only a few years longer, but oh! such glorious years! If I die long before my time, what adventures will I sacrifice? What tender loves and kisses will I not experience? What successes and failures will I not be able to pass to my grandchildren? How can I turn my back on such warmth and pleasures? On the other hand, how can I give up this blazing opportunity of instant fame and fortune? If I accept, I will know the magic of flying to my dying days, and I will have Ivan by my side. If I refuse, I will live a long life—or perhaps be run

over by a bus tomorrow morni
it?"

"Yes."

It was an agonizing deci
agreed, ambivalence lingerin
right. I will respect your final wish. I will accep
the gift ... and I will pay the price. But how is this
done—this transfer?"

"It is done simply, and will require but a few
seconds of discomfort. We will lie here clinging
tightly to one another. Your body will tingle and
spasm during the short time it takes the energy
mass to enter and adjust. After a few minutes, my
life forces will be completely drained. I will then
die, and you will have the power to dance above
the stage. "Now kiss me—firmly—to begin the
process."

They lay side by side on the grassy knoll and
pressed their bodies together, each holding the
other tightly. When he felt Tanyika begin to
shudder, Rodenski said, "You have brought me
much pleasure these past months and I will be
eternally grateful. Do not grieve for me when I
... am ... gone ..."

Tanyika felt his arms slacken. His head
dropped back and his limp body rolled onto its
back.

"*No*," she cried, shaking his lifeless head.
"Please don't go." But when she looked into his

pen eyes she knew it was over. She wept over body for a long time, praying for a peaceful eternity for this incredible man.

Ivan, uneasy that Tanyika was taking so long to rejoin him in the rehearsal studio, returned to the stage in time to watch the final moments of the drama. When he saw Tanny kneeling and weeping over the prone body of Rodenski, he stepped out from the wings. "Tanny, what's wrong?"

She jumped up and put her arms around her lover's neck. "Oh Ivan, I have such exciting news! Come dance with me while I tell you the most wonderful story."

She took him firmly by the hands and began twirling him. Faster and faster, until she lifted him from the stage.

PAYBACK

▼

The old woman leaned over, lowered her mop and bucket to the concrete landing, then grunted as she struggled to pull open the heavy church door. When she had opened it far enough, she propped it with a foot to keep it from closing. She leaned over to retrieve her implements, shuffled through, and let the door swing shut behind her.

"Somebody's gonna hear about this," she mumbled. "That side door ain't supposed to be locked, an' I ain't supposed to be comin' in through the front."

She paused and glanced around the sanctuary. The church was empty this early on a Saturday morning, giving her a moment to enjoy the silence. She'd worked there so long the icons and artifacts no longer held her in awe, and the stained glass windows were but pretty pieces of colored glass. Besides, she had been in and out so many times, she saw the church mainly as a complicated cleaning job—surfaces to dust, things to move, ladders to climb, floors to mop.

But the silence—that was special. She didn't get to experience much of that in her bustling house, filled as it was with grandchildren unable to speak without shouting. "Grand Central is what it is," she muttered.

Resuming her journey, she shuffled toward the altar in her worn loafers, scuffing heels as she moved. Half way to her destination, she suddenly stopped and lowered the bucket to the floor. Bowing her head in thought, she said, "Did I just see somethin' in one of them pews?"

She turned and retraced her steps, sighing. There, on a pew in the fifth row from the back. A sleeping body. Prodding the inert form with the mop handle, she said, "Here now. You can't be sleepin' in them pews. The preacher don't like folks using his church for no hotel." Detecting no movement, she prodded and called again. Still no response. Shuffling along the pew, she shook the foot closest to her.

Nothing. Without changing expression, she said, "Are you dead?" Sniffing the air, she wrinkled her nose at the slight odor of decay and said, "Whew! Of course you are. But you can't stay there, you know," she said, sternly. "There's gonna be people showin' up in a few minutes and they ain't gonna stand for no dead bodies in the pews. And let me tell you, girlie, for the pittance they pay me to clean this place, it don't cover no body hauling, neither."

With no reaction from the corpse, the old woman sighed again. "Well, all right. Mebbe just this once, but only 'cause I gotta get you out of sight before the folks show up."

She rolled the young girl to the floor, took hold of the limp arms and pulled. It was hard work, but the feel of the wrists in her hands triggered memories of her glory days as a catcher on the high trapeze. She was plenty strong then, easily catching all but the heaviest of the flyers. In her mind, she could still hear the roar of the crowds. She looked at her hands, half expecting to see palms covered with chalk. A faint smile formed as she was reminded of her stint as a mortuary assistant. There had been no shortage of bodies to wrangle in *that* dreary place, so it hadn't taken long to learn the easiest ways to move them from here to there.

But that was then. Tugging and grunting, she pulled her burden into the aisle nearest the windows and wrestled it down the gentle slope toward the altar. Glancing at her old Mickey Mouse watch, she muttered, "I never did understand why Sunday sermons is held on Saturdays."

Pausing to catch her breath, she noticed the confessional booths. An idea formed. "Perfect!" she said, and set to work. She opened the ornate door, and ran a hand over the velvet upholstery of the priest's chair. "Chair," she harrumphed. "Looks more like the throne of the king of England." She had no idea what that, or any other, throne looked like, but this chair looked like one to her just the same.

Returning to her task, she grasped the body under the armpits and dragged it into the booth. Grunting with the effort, she wrestled the still-warm corpse onto the "throne." Stretching to her full height, she arched her back while reviewing her handiwork. Shaking her head, she mumbled, "No. This ain't right. Nobody goes in here but the priest." She dragged the body out again. Opening the door to the penitents' booth, she repeated her actions and arranged the corpse on the bench.

"There," she said, grinning at her handiwork. "*That* ought'a give that pervert preacher somethin' to think about besides them innocent choir boys."

But scanning her new scene made her shake her head. "This won't do. She looks too much like a sleeping beauty just dropped in for a nap." Acting on a sudden inspiration, she tugged off the young girl's panties and draped them over her ankles. Next, she tore the blouse apart. "Poor thing musta' been stabbed." She tore the bra apart and pulled it aside to expose blood-stained breasts. Then, pulling up the short skirt and spreading the stiffening legs, she cackled. "There. I'd call that a good day's work."

Retrieving a dust-cloth from a pocket of her smock—it had been one of her husband's favorite undershirts in earlier years—she wiped everything she thought she had touched. As a final gesture of payback, she pulled strands of the corpse's hair over the face and messed up the rest. "There. Let's see what the old letch has to say about *this*."

Closing the door, she picked up her mop and bucket and shuffled toward the priest's office. Once inside that sound-deadened room, she could barely hear the screams of the shocked parishioners gathering around the horror-filled confessional.

She picked up her feather-duster and began swishing it over the bookshelves. As an afterthought, she reached for the phone and dialed 911.

TOO HOT TO CARE

▼

Head drooping, PFC Barney Wizkowski let his M1 rifle slide to the ground, butt first, then wiped a grimy sleeve across his sweating brow. Sagging to his knees, he cupped his hands over the weapon's muzzle and let his head droop toward his chest. He was relieved the battle was over—for now—but Christ only knew when the next attack would come to slam him back into the middle of hell.

Lifting his head, he scanned the sea of bodies lying in grotesque positions, some draped over dead tree trunks, others with heads buried in the weeds. *Too many. Some ours, some theirs—all dead*.

Sickened by the sight, he hoped the grave detail arrived before dark. If it didn't, the bodies would begin to stink by noon tomorrow.

The forest, though thick enough to shield the ground from the blazing sun, also kept the soggy air from stirring so much as a leaf. In the oppressive heat, the nauseating odors of fresh blood and perforated guts hung in the air like poison gas. His stomach quivered.

Sweat trickled down Barney's back, from under his arms, and off his chin. Taking stock through a haze of jumbled thought, he suddenly realized he had to pee. *How long has it been? Long enough to know I better relieve myself before I wet my pants.* He snorted. *That's a laugh. How can my pants get any wetter than they are?*

Still, not wanting to smell of rancid urine, he fumbled with his fly. With one hand supporting his upright rifle and the other on his whizzer, he closed his eyes and let go, letting his head roll back as relief flooded his body. *Ahh.* He was too hot to care how far he lobbed his stream. "Who gives a shit?" he mumbled.

When he opened his eyes, a German soldier stood next to him, knees sagging and body swaying from fatigue. "Ist hot, ja?"

Is he a mirage? No, can't be. I can smell him from three feet away. Barney nodded. "Ja, ist hot," he echoed, using his pitiful command of the enemy's language.

"We sit, ja?" Pointing to himself, the soldier added, "Hans."

Wizkowski imitated the gesture. "Barney." He rolled off his knees onto his butt and let the rifle drop to the ground. Leaning on one elbow, he thought, *So what if I get mud in the muzzle? I'm out of ammunition and too tired to lift the damned thing.* He waved a hand in a gesture of invitation.

Hans dropped his own rifle beside Barney's, pushed the helmet off his head and watched it *thunk* onto a stone lying beside his worn shoes. He let his body follow it to the ground. Groaning against sore muscles, he stretched out on his back and moaned. "Ach, das ist gut." With effort, he released a canteen from his belt and offered it to the weary American.

"Thanks." Barney struggled to sit up while fumbling with the cap. He put the canteen to his lips and drank. "Aiieeee!" he screamed, quickly spitting out the hot liquid burning his tongue.

"Ist good?"

"Good, my ass!" Barney again rolled onto his knees, spitting and coughing. "What the hell is that stuff?"

"Schnapps." Hans mimed pouring the liquid on an imaginary wound. "Ist gut."

Recovering from his fiery mouth, Barney took stock of his partner-in-hell. *God, this kid can't be more than sixteen years old. They must really be scraping the bottom of the barrel. He doesn't even have a complete uniform … and those things on his feet look more like worn-out bedroom slippers than boots. I wonder if he's ever fired that rifle.*

Barney reached into his shirt pocket, took out the small roll of "emergency" toilet paper, then reached deeper for a soggy Hershey bar. He held it toward his neighbor. "Chocolate … good," he said, rubbing a hand in a circle over his belly.

The young soldier hesitated, then took the small item and tore at the wrapping with his teeth. "Danke." Mouth full of chocolate, he felt his pockets as though hunting for a suitable gift to offer in return. Finding nothing but family photos, he reached for his rifle and thrust it at his benefactor. "You keep."

Too exhausted to be surprised, Barney took the rifle and pulled back the bolt. *Jeezus, the damned thing's loaded. Wonder why he didn't kill me.* He worked the bolt until all cartridges were ejected, then laid the weapon on the grass between them.

Reaching into another shirt pocket, Barney extracted a half-crumpled package of Lucky Strikes and extended it toward his bedraggled enemy.

"Danke," Hans said, working a bent cigarette from the mangled pack, then offering to return it.

"Keep it," Barney said, waving away the offer.

A sudden wind startled them into looking up at the undulating forest canopy above. Dangling branches, shredded bare by artillery shells, swayed like deadly pendulums, their jagged ends waiting to impale an unlucky soldier slogging his way to who-knows-where.

The breeze gusted, causing loosened branches to shriek like banshees as they plummeted toward the ground.

Shit! It ain't enough we got the enemy in front and artillery shells exploding above, now the goddamned trees are attacking us, too. Wizkowski whipped his helmet on, knowing full well it offered no more protection against the falling javelins than a paper bag.

A few minutes passed in silent, mutual companionship before Barney became aware of muffled voices moving among the trees. When they drifted closer, he was elated to realize they were speaking English. It could be a trick, but he was too hot to care. He stood and waved his hands. "Hey, you guys, over here."

The voices stopped. As one, the figures dropped to their knees and pointed their weapons in his direction. A sergeant wearing a 35th Infantry Division shoulder patch rose from the weeds and approached, weapon aimed.

"Password," he said.

"Betty Grable."

"Keep yer voice down! The Krauts are right over that rise. Hands where we can see 'em."

Barney helped the young soldier to his feet and motioned for him to raise his arms. When he did the same, he waved at the dozen soldiers kneeling with weapons raised. "It's okay, I'm from the point patrol up ahead."

"What the hell you doin' with a Kraut?"

"He just showed up while I was waitin' for you guys. Like I said, I'm with the point patrol up ahead." He reached into his tunic for a map and handed it to the non-com. "I can show you where they're at."

"I asked you what you're doin' with the Kraut."

"I told you—he just showed up and gave me his rifle. Hey, does that mean he's my prisoner?"

"*Prisoner?* You know damned well we can't take prisoners in the middle of a battle."

"What am I supposed to do with him?"

"You *know* what you're supposed to do with him. You can't leave an enemy running around loose behind the lines—it ain't safe. He could grab a weapon from any one of those bodies and raise all kinds of hell."

Barney shook his head. "I ... I can't do it."

"Why the hell not? Yer a soldier, ain'cha?"

"I'm ... I'm out of ammo."

"Oh, fer Christ's sake." The sergeant spat on the ground. "Here's some ammo," he growled, handing Barney a loaded, eight-round .30-06 clip for his rifle. "Now take him behind those bushes over there and do what you gotta do. And do it *fast*—we gotta keep moving."

Barney stared at the clip of ammo. "He's a POW, for God's sake! Can't I just walk him back to the nearest aid station and leave him there?"

"*What* aid station? We're in the middle of nowhere and the Krauts are getting ready to come at us again. All hell is about to break loose, so *git*."

Tears streaming down his muddy cheeks, Hans seemed to understand the fate awaiting him. He pointed to his shirt pocket, then to his chest.

Understanding the gesture, Barney took the family snapshots from Hans' pocket and reached inside his shirt for the unfinished letter he knew would be there. "I ... promise to get ... these ... to your family." He tried to say more, but his voice cracked. "I'm sorry. We could have been friends."

He picked up his rifle, jammed the clip home without breaking his thumb, and herded his doomed prisoner toward the bushes. The sharp crack of a rifle report pierced the stifling air. As the sound of his shot echoed through the trees, Barney knew he would forever wonder whether he did the right thing. Wiping his eyes, he hurried to catch up to his squad.

As dusk began to fade the forest light, Hans stood and looked out from the bushes in which he had hidden, just as a young GI suddenly hove into view.

Startled by the unexpected sight of an enemy uniform, the frightened GI hurriedly raised his rifle and fired until the German soldier staggered and dropped from view.

THE MISSION

▼

He seemed awfully mature for a thirteen-year-old boy, but his teacher had seen bigger, so didn't give it much thought. Except for his hair—coal-black, thick, and shiny. Still, there was something different about him. Not like others of his age group—active, fidgety, playful—he remained always quiet, polite, helpful, and focused. God, was he focused! His attention span challenged that of highly educated adults. Even his name—Tomso—was unusual. *But I'm glad he was assigned to my class.*

Against her best intentions, she found herself watching him stroll around the playground during recess. He didn't interact much with the other kids. Without being aloof or hostile, he just avoided the boisterous activities of the young. It was as if he were too old for their "running around" games. Yet, if someone offered a game of chess, or asked his help with a math problem, he was always eager to oblige.

Then she froze—*I'm not thinking of him as a "child," but an adult.* That bothered her.

How odd, she thought. *He seems the perfect gentleman. If he were my age I'd try to lure him into asking me for a date.* Idly she wondered, *What it would be like to kiss him? Would he do that with as much intensity he does everything else?* She reddened. The subsequent thoughts sent her scurrying back to the school building. The recess bell ended her reverie.

The following day she watched her students dribbling back to the classroom from recess, bubbling with laughter and high spirits. Maybe the warm spring day made it difficult for them to settle down again. Maybe the prospect of the imminent arithmetic test. She snorted. *Yeah, right!*

When they finally calmed and quieted, she distributed the single page of problems, then wandered around the room to keep order and check on their work.

She glanced at Tomso, and noticed him leaning back in his chair, arms folded, pencil atop his page of problems.

She stopped and looked down at the neatly-groomed boy. His straight black hair glistened, as thick and shiny as ever. She imagined what it would be like to run her fingers through that masculine mane.

"Aren't you going to do the problems I just gave you?"

"Did 'em, Miss Tara." He waved a hand at the page.

"You're finished already?" She felt her eyebrows shoot up. Maybe she was wrong, but it seemed she handed him the assignment barely seconds ago.

"Yes. They were easy." After hesitating, he added, "I'll be glad to do some more, if you'd like. They're fun." Then he frowned as he handed her the sheet.

Does he think he's done something wrong? It took only a glance to verify his answers were all correct. They always were.

On impulse, she decided to act on an idea she'd been toying with for the last two days. "Come to the blackboard with me, Tomso. I'd like to show you a few problems while the others are working."

"I'd like that." He followed her to the front of the room, where she began writing. Pointing to what she had written, "Do you know what this means?"

"Square root of eighty-one. The root is nine."

"You didn't even have to think about that, did you?"

"No, Ma'am."

"Where did you learn about the square root sign?"

Tomso hesitated. It wouldn't do to tell her the answer to *that* question. At least, not yet. "I ... I don't know. Maybe I read about it in a math book from the library."

"Uh-huh." Without writing, she asked, do you happen to know the square root of 1756?"

"It's 41.904653."

"Can you tell me how you worked it out?"

"I didn't have to. As soon as you said the number, the answer was in my mind."

She nodded, controlling her rising excitement. *My God, his math ability is far beyond his years.* Determined to test the limits of his skill, she offered problems in algebra, quadratic equations, and more. She even wrote a few calculus problems, which stretched the outer edge of her own mathematical prowess.

He solved them all in a wink.

"Well, there doesn't seem to be any math problem you can't solve. Would you be willing to work with me again tomorrow? I'd like to check something in the library."

"I'd be glad to."

Tara decided to keep her discovery to herself, at least until she could probe his remarkable talent further. She was itchy curious to know if there was indeed a limit to his intellect, and where it was.

That evening, she buried herself in the library stacks, then returned to her apartment to scour the Internet.

The next day, as her students struggled with the assigned problems, she called Tomso to her desk. Unfolding a star chart, she placed a forefinger on each of two stars. "Do you know how someone would go about calculating the distance between Ganymede and Sirius?" She was certain he'd never even heard of those stars, let alone know how to calculate interstellar distances. She was wrong.

Tomso nodded, bent toward the map for a closer look, and explained how such a problem could be solved.

Tara was speechless. *This is impossible. There's no way a thirteen-year-old boy could be this knowledgeable.* Then she gasped as she heard him mutter, "But the natives don't call it Ganymede."

It took all her will power to keep from shouting the news about Tomso to everyone she met. To strengthen her resolve, she thought about the consequences of sharing her exciting discovery. *I'm bursting to tell somebody about him, but if I did, they'd turn him into some kind of a freak. They'd have him performing his math "tricks" for assembled mathematicians and astronomers, then put him on television. That would be even worse than putting him into a circus ... and you* know *that's what they'd do, don't you? Especially if he let slip something like his comment about the natives of Ganymede. So keep your mouth shut. Besides, what if he knows as much about every other subject as he does about math and astronomy?"* Still thrilling with excitement, she vowed to keep the secret awhile longer.

Calmed by her monologue, she returned to the library for another study session. She worked until the librarian told her, "Closing time. Sorry."

The next day, she invited Tomso to stay after school when everyone left. As soon as the building was empty, she took him to the now-vacant teacher's lounge. There, she asked him to sit on the sofa and pulled a chair up close, facing him. Uncertain where to begin, she decided to start with the truth.

"Tomso, your abilities truly amaze me, and I'd like to learn more about you. Do you mind?"

"Not at all." Since they were alone, he reached out and touched the back of her hand.

A ripple, as of electricity, ran up her arm and seemed to sparkle throughout her nervous system. Goosebumps sprouted. She tingled all over. Though all aquiver, she managed to say, "Tomso, do you realize how unusual you are?"

"Yes, Ma'am. I try to hide it, but every once in awhile I can't help it—like when I finished that page of practice problems too quickly. I shouldn't have done that."

"Is that why you don't want to be put into an advanced class, or skipped a grade or two? Because you're trying to blend in?

He nodded. "Yes. I would stand out because I'd be brighter than the others, but smaller and younger."

"You really are quick at grasping things. Yes, those would be the disadvantages." She groped for a reasonable approach. "Do you have a preference, or a different idea? What would you like *me* to do?"

"Oh, I've thought about it, of course. For now, I'd like to stay right where I am. I promise to try harder to make myself fit in. Maybe you can show me how to do that."

He reached out and took her hands in his while looking deep into her eyes.

Within seconds, she drifted down, down, down … into a deep, sleep-like unconsciousness. An overwhelming sense of warmth, and comfort, and safety crept over her … then her dreams began.

At first, she floated on a pink cloud. After only a few seconds she felt hands caressing her body. Delicate fingers ran up and down her arms, then along her thighs.

God, they felt good! Like nothing she had ever known. Another few seconds and she felt curiously refreshed … and satisfied. She opened her eyes to see whose hands they were. She didn't really care that much, only how wonderful they made her feel. And, dreamily, she found herself still staring into Tomso's expressionless face.

She felt him unfastening the buttons of her blouse. In her dreamy state, it seemed as if they had been doing this forever, and she reached up her hands to help. But the dream faded away.

She awakened, lying on the cot in the teacher's lounge, wondering how and when she got there. All she could remember was sitting across from Tomso and looking into his eyes. Yet, she knew something else happened too. What was it? Oh, yes, something about the buttons on her blouse.

Abruptly she leaped to her feet. *Did he …?* She reached down and reached under her skirt. Her panties were folded and placed beside her on the cot! *Then it* wasn't *just a dream? It really happened? I just had sex with a thirteen-year-old boy! Why am I not alarmed? But it felt so good. I must discuss this with him … but not before I luxuriate a bit longer in these pleasant sensations.*

Returning to the library that evening, she checked out an astrophysics text containing practice problems. She hoped to continue probing Tomso's intellect, but mused, at the same time, over how best to approach today's incident. She decided tomorrow would be soon enough to sort it all out.

The next day, he answered all the questions and solved all the problems perfectly. Somehow, she knew he would.

Again, at her request, Tomso lingered after the others had gone for the day. "Would you like to continue our little experiment?" he asked.

Before she could reply, he took her hand and led her directly to the lounge. Sitting across from her as before, he reached for her hands and looked into her eyes.

As soon as his fingers touched her hand she felt the tingle. It warmed her. She felt so relaxed … so safe. Soon after, the dreams began. This time she floated, as if high in a unique sky, on a blue cloud, sipping on a straw dipped into a richly-spiced chocolate soda. When the liquid touched her tongue, she heard music … strange, inspiring, yet alien, music that could only come from somewhere "out there."

Slowly she awakened, lying on the cot as before, unwilling to return to reality, knowing an unearthly satisfaction. Again, her panties were folded and placed beside her.

When she at last stood, she vowed, *I must talk with Tomso about this. This can't go on. It's wrong, wrong, wrong! If we're caught, I'd be arrested for contributing to the delinquency of a minor. I* must *talk to him. This cannot go on any longer.*

But it did—for three weeks more. Addicted to his touch, she always relented.

Finally, she called Tomso to the lounge for what she was determined would be "the last time."

When he reached for her hands, she pulled back. "No," she said, tears beginning to erupt. "We must NOT do this anymore."

Tomso dropped his hands in a gesture of dismay. "Do you not find it pleasurable?"

"Oh, yes! More than anything I've ever experienced. But it is wrong. It must stop."

"All right. We will stop." He smiled and it was as if a great light brightened the darkness. "Miss Tara, it was pleasurable for me also ... but, with you, today, my mission here is complete. My time is up."

"Me? Mission? Here? Your time is up? What do you mean?"

Tomso's smile turned grim. "Here. Earth. My mission has been to impregnate as many qualified young females as time allowed. I have done that. Now I must move on."

Tara's mouth dropped open. "Impregnate? You ... you mean I'm *pregnant?*"

"Yes." He said it without emotion.

She grasped her head in her hands. "I've been impregnated by a thirteen-year-old *boy*? Oh ... my ... God!"

His smile returned. "*No*. By a *man*. Here I simply look like a boy among your kind. On my planet, I am the equivalent of forty-seven years old on earth."

"But why?"

"It was our mission to improve the breeding stock of your planet ... so you will become less destructive and more civilized."

Tara was dumbfounded, confused. "*Breeding* stock? You mean you've impregnated others, too?" She sobbed quietly as the implications of his message seeped into her consciousness.

"Please try to understand. It is my duty to my world. I am sorry if I have embarrassed you in any way. It was not my intention.

"But ... but ... will I ever see you again?"

"Yes. I will come to you in your dreams ... and, eventually, through the eyes of your beautiful twins, a boy and girl. And, so you can quit teaching if you wish, go to some lovely place of your dreams, and avoid any social repercussions while giving our children the love and care they will require, I have placed a large sum of money in your savings account."

"But ... but ..."

"That is all I can tell you for now. Your children's minds will contact your own when they mature in another five years. You will see me again at that time, wherever I may be. Then you will experience your world—and mine—in newer and more exciting ways." He pulled her close and kissed her. "Until then, remember me as warmly as I will remember you."

That final kiss, before he vanished, left Tara floating once more. Only this time she seemed to drift in infinite space, surrounded by all the stars of the universe.

The Inconsiderate Corpse

───────────── ▼ ─────────────

"That corpse is *definitely* out of place," she huffed. "It's not as though the bitch wasn't invited to perform as one of the dancers in my chorus, you know. But to show up and *die*? In a bright red dress and green pumps? Well, *really*! It's just ... *too much*."

The outraged soprano swished her long gown and stomped her foot, making yet another dent in the hardwood stage floor as she continued her rant. "That social-climbing trollop knew perfectly well that *I'm* supposed to be the focus of attention. I've no doubt she died right there in front of the footlights just to spite me. I swear I will *never* speak to her again!" She bashed a closed fist into her palm to underscore the point.

The rumpled inspector scratched the side of his bulbous nose with the back end of a ball-point pen, then scratched a few words in his notebook. "I take it you weren't fond of the deceased, Miss Farnsworth?"

"Certainly not! She was a snotty little tramp who always wore the wrong color nail polish. If I'd known she was going to *die* just to be the center of attention, I wouldn't have given her a part, *would* I?"

"Why do you think she died on the stage?" He spoke while thinking, *What a self-centered airhead.*

"To ruin my performance, of course. Why else?"

"Uh-huh." The inspector peeked over his glasses, scratched his balding head, and made another note. "Maybe she had a heart attack."

"If she did, it was self-induced. She's the type who'd do *anything* for attention."

"Did she have any enemies—besides you, that is?"

"I *beg* your pardon! I didn't like her—I admit that—but I wouldn't consider myself her enemy. It's just that she was ... well, insufferable."

"But still, you asked her to sing in your chorus."

"Of *course!*" she blurted, as though the reason for her invitation was self-explanatory. "Mimi

Malone was very well-connected on the social scene. It's considered a feather in your cap to have her in your cast—no matter how small the part."

"Even though you considered her insufferable?"

"Of course!"

"And dead?"

"That has nothing to do with it. She had *connections.*"

"I see." The inspector shook his head. The singer hated the woman, yet invited her to appear in the performance. Prominent socialite or not, something didn't smell right. He rubbed his reddening nose, and suddenly knew what it was. The *flowers.* The damned flowers! The stage was full of them and they always reminded him of funerals. Worse, they irritated his sinuses and made his eyes water. He wiped them with the rumpled handkerchief he tugged from a pocket, all the while holding a finger under his nose to keep from sneezing.

"Please, sit over there on that bench for a few minutes," he said. Pointing toward himself, he said, "Now that the crime scene gnomes have gone, it is time for *me* to investigate."

Settling herself on the bench, the frustrated soprano snorted. "I don't know what you hope to find, inspector. It's as plain as the nose on your face. She died to spite me. What more do you need to know?"

Already weary of the carping prima donna, the inspector turned to the body. He was glad that, after names and addresses had been duly recorded, he had encouraged the remaining audience and cast members to leave. The relative silence helped him think.

The inspector snapped on a pair of surgical gloves and kneeled beside the body, quickly noticing the conspicuous absence of blood, bullet holes, or knife wounds. The only visible injury seemed to be a scratch on the left breast of the deceased. "No doubt incurred when the generous mound plopped loose from its mooring as she fell," he muttered.

Moving toward the lower extremities, he lifted the bright red dress to discover whatever clues might lie beneath. His eyesight not what it once was, he touched the pink garter to make sure it wasn't merely a tattoo. *Do women still wear garters?* he wondered. *How quaint. Perhaps they are an ancient theatrical lucky charm.* On moving the garter an inch to one side, he noticed the reddened flesh under and around the item in question. Trying hard to avoid a sneeze—it didn't work—he lobbed a comment at the fuming singer. "Is every female in the chorus supposed to wear a garter?"

"Don't tell me that little slut is wearing one, too? That is just too, too much! Is it a white one, like mine?"

"Actually, it's pink, with a little red lace trim." He removed the garter from the immobile leg and held it up.

"That's *it!*" screamed the prima donna as she leaped from the bench. "I'll kill her myself. I don't care if she *is* already dead."

The inspector restrained her barely in time to stop her from letting fly with the tip of a shoe. "May I see *your* garter?" he asked.

"What for? You some kind of pervert?"

The inspector ignored the insult, having been called worse. Reaching out an open hand, he repeated his request. "Please?"

The outraged woman lifted her gown, pulled a garter from her leg, and threw it at the inspector. "There! See if you can get off on *that.*"

Pinching the garter between thumb and forefinger, the inspector slowly wafted it under his nose, wrinkling it as he did so. "Ah ... ah ... a-choo!" The sneeze ricocheted around the walls of the near-empty theater. When finished wiping his reddening proboscis, he breathed deeply to regain his composure. Then, standing like a soldier about to be pinned with a medal, he intoned, "Marylee Farnsworth, I arrest you for the murder of ... of Miss Mimi Malone." He whirled the surprised woman around and handcuffed her hands behind her back.

This action triggered screaming epithets, wads of spit, and a brace of kicks to his shins. "How dare you accuse me of murder? Why, I've never so much as met that woman before today!"

When the rant subsided, the inspector held a garter in each hand, as far from his nose as his arms would allow. "Oh, come now, Miss Farnsworth," he chided. You say you've never met Miss Malone before today?"

"Absolutely not."

"Yet you found her insufferable? How, may I ask, could you find her insufferable if you didn't even know her?"

"She ... she simply *was! Everybody* knows it."

"You may turn off the histrionics and the lies, Miss Farnsworth. The charade is over."

With finger raised, the inspector orated as he paced. "When I was introduced to you on entering the theater, I found it almost impossible to keep from sneezing. At first, I thought it was the flowers. I became puzzled when I scanned the stage and didn't see any gardenias—that's what I'm allergic to. Then, when I lifted the dress of the corpse and fingered the garter, I *did* sneeze, from which I concluded the garter had been soaked in gardenia perfume ... just like *your* garter, Miss Farnsworth."

"That's silly. *Anybody* can buy that perfume."

"That may be so, but it is something of a coincidence, don't you think? Of all the fragrances in the world, that your supporting singer's garter should be soaked in the same perfume as your own?"

"Oh, for heaven's sake, inspector. They weren't *soaked* in it. Besides, what if they were?"

He whirled and pointed a finger in her direction. "Aha! Then you *knew* the corpse was wearing such an item, did you not? Did you present your little poisoned gift in the Green Room before the performance began?"

"Poisoned?"

"Yes, poisoned. Look for yourself." With a flourish, the inspector pulled up the dress of the deceased, revealing the ring of blistered flesh where the garter had clung. "The poison allowed the victim to get as far as center stage before doing its work, but no further. From the speed of its action and the pinkish skin, my guess is nicotine, laced with a generous dollop of cyanide." Turning toward the defiant killer, he said, "Did you think Miss Malone would be safely away before she finally died somewhere else?"

Farnsworth pushed her lower lip forward and stomped a foot. "That snobby hussy snubbed me for *years* before condescending to join my cast, then dared to show her face in that garish red dress. Mere dying was much too good for her."

"As I thought. But there is something else." He held the garters under her nose, again as far from his own as possible. "It is true that one is pink and one is white, but that is the extent of their differences. That, my dear lady, is the final proof this poisoned garter could only have been provided by *you*."

"How can that prove anything? There must be millions of garters like mine."

"Oh, my dear madam, the probability of that being true must be much too small to calculate. You see, they're both embroidered with your name. Why would the deceased wear a garter inscribed with *your* name?"

"Who knows what she's capable of? You think the world isn't full of Marylees?"

"Perhaps so. But there is also the matter of the label." He held the garters under her nose and nodded toward the tiny label sown on the underside of each.

They read, "Hand-fashioned for Marylee—my favorite soprano—by your Aunt Maude, 1995."

The Awakening

▼ ————————

At the first touch of a cool, moist towel against her face, Carla struggled to lift her eyelids. It didn't work. The thin sliver of light seeping into her swollen eyes revealed only a blur. And the effort exhausted her shallow well of energy. And God, how she hurt.

Sighing, she resolved to try again later. Much later.

Opening her eyes wasn't the only painful act she attempted. *Any* activity made lightning bolts shoot in so many directions she longed to return to unconsciousness.

Carla eased back into the world again two days later. Again, a cool, wet cloth stroked her head and neck. *Oh, how good that feels!* she thought. It reminded her of the time, as a young teenager, she screamed her way home from the beach wearing a searing sunburn. Her mother's soothing voice and cool damp towel had removed the sting better than any medicine she could have imagined.

Taking stock of her present condition, she noted the worst of the pain had subsided. This time, when she opened her swollen eyes as far as she was able, she saw a shiny pin-point of light surrounded by the hazy form of a woman with white hair. She opened her mouth to speak.

"Don't try to talk yet," crooned a soft voice reminding Carla of warm maple syrup. "We can talk in another day or two."

Even so, Carla tried. "Day?"

"Today's Wednesday. You entered the hospital on Sunday. Now don't talk."

"You ... angel?"

"No, my dear, I'm just a volunteer. Now get some rest."

The broken woman pointed an unsteady finger at the shiny object around her benefactor's neck. "No! Angel."

"Oh, this charm?" She fingered the odd-shaped item hanging on the fine silver chain. "I'll tell you all about it when you're better. Now rest."

Friday morning, Carla again wakened to feel the cool cloth stroking her head and neck. Cracking her eyelids, she focused at once on the kind, motherly face before her—and the peculiar pendant hanging at her neck.

She tried to smile, but it still hurt. "That feels good. Your name?"

"Emily. Emily Strang."

"Feeling ... better. Thirsty ... hungry."

Emily smiled a grandmotherly smile and squeezed Carla's hand. "That's good. I'll bring you some orange juice and something solid."

She glided from the room. When she returned, she fed Carla with a tenderness Carla hadn't known for years.

"There," Emily said. "That should help get your strength back."

Carla blinked her eyes in agreement.

When Emily arrived the following Monday, she asked, "Feeling better today? Weekend restful?"

Carla grinned as she nodded.

Emily rearranged the bed and fussed over Carla's pillow. "Up for a little talk?"

"Yes."

"Can you tell me how this happened to you?"

"Fuh ... fell down stairs."

"Uh-huh. That happened to me a few times in my earlier life, too. Tell me, do you have a two-story house?" Emily asked.

"No ... ranch." Caught in her lie, Carla's face reddened.

"That's all right, sweetie. We've nursed many women like you back to health. Trouble is, when they recover, they're usually back in a month or two. But, don't worry. I had the same problem myself a few years back. Would you like to talk about it?"

Carla's brows furrowed. Her teeth clenched. Her fists balled until the knuckles turned white. "Yes ... talk," she said, her voice a mixture of whisper and gurgle. "First, tell ... *your* story."

"All right. But you relax while I talk. You can ask questions later."

A small nod signaled acquiescence.

"I was married to a prosperous businessman," Emily began. "As he expanded his services—he was a workaholic, you see—business got even better. That led to more and more stress. I tried to ease his strain by helping with the business, and for a while we were happy. Then gradually, he changed. At first, nothing I did was good enough for him. He shouted a lot and treated me like a worthless employee. Then he began insulting and belittling me. He even isolated me from my friends. Finally, he began hitting me. Oh, he was peaches and cream in front of others, but when we were alone he would beat me harder and harder. One day he beat me so bad I found myself right where you are today."

Carla must have noticed Emily's eyes glistening. She raised a forearm to interrupt. "What ... what did you ... do?"

"A week after I got home from the hospital he packed his bags and disappeared. I began running the business myself. I already knew how to handle most of the tasks and the rest I learned by 'stumble and bumble.'" Emily paused to choose her next words. "He never came back. I was glad. It gave me time to heal and recover my self-respect. To tell the truth, my dear, since then I've been having the time of my life."

"Not sorry ... he's gone?"

"Sorry? No. I know he would have killed me if I hadn't—if he hadn't disappeared. No, I'm not one bit sorry."

"Did you have him declared dead?"

"I didn't bother. I reported him missing and the police made out a report. But I only made a feeble effort to find him. I knew if he came back, he'd start beating me again. In my heart, I knew he'd soon kill me."

"I'm so sorry ..."

Emily smiled. "I'm not. Fortunately, he'd put everything in my name early on, so creditors would find it hard to collect anything from him—he owed half the people in town. Because everything was already mine when he left, I simply took up where he left off."

"The police didn't—?"

"No. After I reported him missing that was the last I heard of it."

Carla stared at the ceiling, lost in thought. "Wish I could ..."

Emily turned to leave and a nurse entered the room. She moved close to Emily and whispered, "Her husband was here again, clamoring to see his wife."

"I thought this was posted as a 'No Visitors' room."

"It is, but he was being insistent. The sonuvabitch even had the nerve to bring flowers."

"Did you call security?"

"Of course. They escorted him from the building. Carla is in no condition to have visitors, least of all her husband." She eyed Carla. "Has she told you what happened?"

"Not yet. She's still pretty shaky."

Pretending otherwise, Carla overheard every word. But rather than cringing in fear at the thought of facing her tormentor, her jaw set and her hands balled into fists. She looked at those fists, surprised at her defiant reaction. *"Never again,"* she whispered, and drifted off to sleep.

Carla had combed her hair and added a bit of lipstick by the time Emily arrived the following morning. "How did my husband react when you wouldn't let him in?"

"Oh. You heard about that? He got pretty belligerent when we told him 'No Visitors' meant just that. Claimed he was going to sue the hospital."

"How typical."

"You can have him put in jail, you know."

"*No!* I don't want him in jail. I want him dead! It's the only way I can be totally free of him. If he's in jail, he'll get out, and then he'll find me and kill me. Then do it to someone else. I just *know* it!"

"Have you thought of leaving him?"

"A thousand times. But if I did, he'd find me. He'd bring me flowers and apologize, and promise never to do it again. Before long, he'd start hitting me again—this is the third time he's put me into this hospital—but he'd *never* let me go. You see, like your husband, he put everything in my name, too. If I left him, he'd *have* to find me."

"Suppose ... just suppose ... he disappeared forever?"

"Like your husband?"

"Exactly."

"That would be wonderful. But how could such a miracle happen?"

"All things are possible. Now get a good night's sleep and we'll talk tomorrow."

That night Carla fought the sedative-induced drowsiness. There were too many exciting things to think about. She thrilled at the vision of a new life without her brutal husband. She warmed at the prospect of sliding into bed each night without the fear of another round of humiliation and beating. She saw herself rising each morning and wandering around the house in robe and slippers with no one to criticize her "insufferable laziness." She visualized herself choosing the clothing she wore ... and her own friends. She even imagined having her own dog to love—a faithful companion to love her in return.

But is such a thing possible? If I filed for divorce, he'd make my life even more of an inferno than it already is. If I left him in the middle of the night, he'd find me, and kill me. I just can't think of an option that would work! *But Emily implied she knows a way.*

Caressing that hope, she drifted off to sleep.

The next morning, Carla embarked on the adventure of shuffling to the bathroom on her own. Gazing at the facial scars of beatings past, she washed her face and brushed her teeth, savoring each small accomplishment as a major triumph. She snickered as she imagined herself standing on an Olympic podium accepting a gold medal for the popular and challenging "Teeth-Brushing Event."

Hair combed and makeup applied by the time the trays arrived, she finished off her entire breakfast. She then fluffed her own pillows and straightened her bed.

Emily strolled in for her daily visit right on time. Dressed in her volunteer uniform, she wore that odd pendant along with a small flower in her hair.

Carla was bursting to talk. "Know what I did this morning?" She spread her arms in triumph and described her adventure.

"That's marvelous," Emily replied, "but don't tell the nurse. You're not supposed to do a 'first ambulation' without help."

"I won't tell. But you promised to tell—"

"Yes, I did. In turn, *you* must promise never to reveal what we talk about today."

"I promise. I stayed awake last night trying to think of an answer, but couldn't."

Emily smoothed the skirt of her gray uniform. "Before I begin, do you have any children?"

"No. The beast wouldn't even discuss it."

"Does your husband have an insurance policy on his life?"

"Not that I know of. Why?"

"They won't pay off until your husband is declared dead, you know. That might not happen for seven years." Emily frowned and bent closer. "You say all his assets are in your name?"

"Yes."

"Then what do you imagine would happen if he packed his bags and left?

"Well ... I guess I'd wonder how long it would be before he returned and—"

"I meant if he left forever?"

"How could I *know* that?"

Emily leaned closer. "There's a way, my dear, there's a way."

Carla hesitated. "I ... uh ... wouldn't want him to disappear before I made sure he learned what it feels like to—"

"I understand, and if you don't mind my saying so, you are quite a different person from the one they brought in here ten days ago."

"I feel that, too. Something happened when I was unconscious and in pain," Carla said. "I saw myself drifting away from my body. When I looked down, I saw a pitiful sight. I knelt on the ground, cowering, crying, and pleading for my life. My husband stood over me growling insults ... and hitting me with his baseball bat. Every time he hit me I screamed and begged him to stop. But he didn't." She paused to catch her breath.

"I hated seeing what I'd become. I was nothing but a whimpering slave who would do *anything* to appease my tormentor. I would give up *anything* just to make my sadistic husband happy."

Carla paused again and looked out the window into the sunlight, then shook her head in disbelief.

"I was an appeaser. I tolerated any slight or indignity, endured *anything* and everything to keep from facing the bully and fighting back."

"Did you wake up then?"

"Oh, no. When I was completely consumed with loathing for the pitiful woman I was watching, a white light appeared. First it was just a bright spot in the distance, but it came closer and closer. Somehow, I didn't fear it ... actually, I welcomed it. When it wrapped itself around me, I took it as a sign I didn't have to be the way I was ... I could stand up, raise my head and shout, '*Never again!*' When my husband dropped his bat and faded into the distance, my pain subsided. When I rose from my knees, I felt stronger yet."

"That was quite a dream."

"It *wasn't* a dream, Emily. It was my soul crying out for me to take back my life! When my husband faded from view, I realized I didn't have to go on as I had. I could fight back. This may sound foolish, but I felt as though I could fight the whole world—and win! I'd been transformed, you see. I suppose you can say that at that instant, this worm *turned*."

Emily's eyes gleamed as she squeezed Carla's hand. "That was a very moving experience, my dear. Your expression tells me you did, indeed, experience a transformation. I don't know what caused your vision, but I'm glad it happened. And now I know you'll be fine. Just fine."

"I feel that, too. I'm ready to take back my life, Emily."

"Does that mean you won't be going home when you leave here?"

Carla sat up and slammed a fist into the bed. "Oh, no! I'm going *back* to that house of torture and I'm going to pretend to be the same wimpy doormat I was when I left. Then, when I'm ready, I'm going to take back my life."

"Don't do anything you might later regret."

"Regret? *Regret*? After what I've been through? How could I do *anything* I might regret? I only regret taking this long to stand up to fight for my self-respect—and my dignity as a woman. You said you can show me how. Will you?"

For the next thirty minutes the two locked themselves in hushed conversation. When Emily finished, she whispered, "Be careful. Here's my phone number. You'll know when to use it."

The next morning, Emily wheeled Carla from the hospital and into the morning sun.

Carla shielded her eyes with a hand and squinted against the light. She breathed deeply to inhale the fragrances of the flower gardens bordering the hospital entrance, her eyes watering with joy. "You know, I didn't expect to live to see this day."

"Yes, it is a wonderful day, but won't it be a shock to your husband if you don't call him before showing up? He's been here every day making a scene when he wasn't allowed in. That's why we posted a policeman at your door."

"I don't care if he screamed his head off. I'm strong now, Emily, and I want to slip home while he's still at work. That'll give me time to shop and make my ... my arrangements."

"You'll look a sight walking into the stores wearing those bandages and sling. You know you don't need them anymore."

"I don't need this wheelchair, either. But it's all part of the plan, Emily ... all part of the plan."

Her benefactor nodded. "All right. I'm off shift now, so the least you can do is let me drive you home."

Emily drove into the driveway Carla indicated and parked her black van. "I really do wish you'd let me help with your shopping."

"Thank you, but I can handle it myself. I *have* to." Carla opened the door and stepped onto the asphalt, her bundle of clothing and hospital remnants tucked under her un-splinted arm. "I can't tell you how much you've meant to me. You really are an angel."

Emily smiled and handed Carla a small plastic bag. "Here's your 'tool bag.' I've included instructions." She patted Carla on the shoulder. "Now go do what you have to do. When it's time, call me."

Entering her empty house, the stinking, rancid odors convinced Carla a leaking garbage truck must have rumbled through. Soiled clothing draped the furniture. The laundry hamper overflowed. Dirty pans and dishes decorated the kitchen sink. Crumbs and remnants of a hasty breakfast lay scattered across the kitchen table.

At first, Carla ignored the domestic chaos. Then she threw off the bandages and sling, changed her clothes and pampered her face with makeup.

Only after returning from a quick trip to the mall and hiding her purchases did she begin work on the house. Oddly, she enjoyed the daunting tasks, even humming as she cleaned. She collected the soiled clothing and, after sorting them, threw the first load into the washer.

The kitchen proved a bigger challenge. She scraped dried food from plates, stuffed spoiled food into the disposal, and ran a full dishwasher—twice. She mopped the grease spots from the stovetop and kitchen floor, all with a determination she hadn't known for years.

Periodically, she bolstered her spirits by reciting her new mantra, "That bastard will be sorry he ever laid a hand on me."

Finally, the cleaning and laundering finished, she treated herself to a long, hot shower, savoring her plans for the evening as she let the welcome liquid roll down her shoulders and back. Drying herself with a thick, fluffy towel twenty minutes later, she powdered her body and added a dab of her favorite perfume. "There. That should attract the fly into my web. I still hurt, but I'm good to go."

Dressing in her black low-cut dress, she completed her costume with a pair of knee-high patent leather boots. She chose the black ones with the high heels.

Inspecting herself in the full-length mirror, she threw herself a kiss and sat at her dressing table to tweak her makeup. "Just a leetle too much lipstick ... and a tad too much rouge. Ta-Da! Now to add a little too much eyebrow pencil. Perfect! A fluff of the hair," she matched action to the words, "and I can whore myself all the way down Main Street." She laughed aloud at the image.

Dancing a two-step in time to music only she heard, Carla next placed her "props" in their assigned places and set the dining room table for dinner. Tablecloth, silver candlestick holders with tall black candles, the special-occasion silverware, and wine glasses that rang when tapped.

"I'm ready for the main event." She held her hands in front of her. "Steady as a rock. By God, I *am* a different woman!"

She then placed the bandage back on her head and the sling back on her arm. Now it was time to raise the curtain: time to deliver the first lines of her performance.

Carla punched a number into her cell and, speaking with her timid voice from her past, told her husband, "Hello, Dale? I'm home."

An hour later his car screeched into the garage. He slammed the car door shut and banged open the door to the house. "Carla? Carla, baby? Is that you?"

She sat at the kitchen table pretending weakness, peeling potatoes. *Same old Dale*, she thought. *He brought flowers ... just as I predicted. As though they'd wipe away ten years of pain and humiliation. Not this time, you vicious beast, not this time!*

Dale laid the bouquet on the table, dropped his briefcase on the floor, and reached out to her. "My God, what happened to you? Are you all right? You really shouldn't have made me hit you like that. You know how I hate it when you make me beat you. But I promise I'll never do it again, Baby. I swear it, Sweetheart."

You can say that again, you Neanderthal! Carla shrank from his embrace, pretending fear. With her voice quivering, she said, "We're having dinner in the dining room tonight. I want to atone for making you so angry again." Her throat choked on the words. "Now please go freshen up while I make things ready. I want them to be just right for you." *The sonuvabitch never even noticed the clean house. Well, it's payback time.*

"All right, Sweetheart. Everything will be just like old times, I promise." Leaving the bouquet lying on the table, he headed for the bedroom.

Carla placed the tomato and cucumber salads on the black placemats and lit the candles. Later, in the kitchen, she struggled with still-sore hands to open the special bottle of red wine she'd purchased earlier that day.

Dale appeared, wearing a light blue polo shirt and slacks, and rushed to her side. "Here, let me help you with that," he said, taking the bottle and its opener from her hands. "Hey! This looks expensive. How much did you pay for it?"

"Please don't be angry with me. This is a special night. If you'll sit down, I'll bring everything to the table."

Following her instructions, he took his place in the dining room.

In the kitchen, Carla poured wine into the two glasses she'd made sparkle for the occasion. Taking a small vial from the coffee can where she'd hidden Emily's gifts, she unscrewed the top and sniffed. *Just as Emily said ... only a slight odor.* While she poured the contents into one of the glasses, she muttered a line from an old Tom Lehrer song, "... and sprinkled just a bit, on each banana split." She swirled the glass containing the additive and carried both to the table, placing the doctored wine in front of her husband.

When seated, she raised her glass as if in a toast. "Here's to better times." She couldn't bear to look at him as she spoke.

"Yes," he echoed, "to better times."

She watched closely when he raised the glass to his lips and drank.

The few words spoken during the salad course were stilted and filled with platitudes. Neither was ready to touch on sensitive subjects.

Carla watched as Dale's hand strayed toward his wine glass again and again, only to move away, as if teasing her. *This is agonizing. Oh, how I wish he'd pick it up and finish it off in one big gulp.*

Sip by sip, the wine was at last consumed. "Another glass, dear?" she asked.

Dale yawned. "I dunno. This glass seems to have hit me pretty hard ... must have had a tougher day than I thought." Dale's eyes drooped.

"Poor baby. Feeling drowsy?"

"Yeah, guess ... so."

That's my cue. The main act is about to begin!

She picked up the empty salad plates and took them to the kitchen counter. She then took a shoebox hidden in a cupboard and placed it on the dining room table. Next, with a dramatic flourish she whipped off her sling and head bandage and threw them into her husband's face.

"Wha' the ... ?"

It pleased Carla to note his difficulty in making his tongue follow orders from his brain. "I've a few surprises for you." In a voice plated with the steel of authority, she continued. "The first one is that I'm no longer the simpering woman you tried to kill—"

"I ... never ... tried—"

"Don't interrupt! As I said, I'm my own woman now, and you'll never again lay a finger on me—or anyone else—ever."

His eyes opened wide before returning to half-mast with the drug's increasing effect.

"Now for the next surprise. Remember how you always wanted to play 'bondage' in the bedroom? How you always wanted to tie me up and do unspeakable things to me? Well, tonight we're going to go all out."

She removed a roll of two-inch duct tape from her shoebox, and with a deftness sprouting from the afternoon's practice session, taped his leaden wrists to the arms of his chair.

"Hey ... wha' the ..."

Carla continued taping his body to the chair, adding two full turns around his arms and torso. "That's just for starters, you bastard."

Returning to her side of the table, she pulled it away from him as far as the room allowed, leaving the drowsy man bound to the chair near the center of the room. A small voice from a corner of her mind whispered, *Are you sure you want to do this? There's no turning back.*

Next, she removed his shoes and socks, and taped each ankle to a chair leg. "Comfy? You want bondage? You're gonna *get* bondage."

Dale now appeared barely awake, but still able to register alarm. He struggled against his bonds, but only managed to make them tighter. Able now to move only his head and mouth, he used his diminishing strength to mumble, "I'll ... kill ... you ... for ... this."

"You've got that just exactly backward, my dear. Just ... exactly ... backward. First, though, we're going to play some bondage games."

She stood back to admire her handiwork. "Wait. Something's missing." She snapped her fingers. "Got it!" She wrapped the tape around his mouth and head—twice. "Can't have you singing bawdy songs while we play, can we?"

She returned the remainder of the duct tape to her box and sprinted to the garage. Reaching under a pile of discarded carpeting, she retrieved a long roll of plastic sheeting, dragged it to the dining room and dropped it beside her abuser's chair. "Now for the first game." She shoved his chair over on its left side.

The bound man toppled with a thump, his head saved from major bruising only by the carpeted floor. "You like that? '*That*,' as you used to say when you knocked me down, 'will get your adrenaline pumping.'"

She unrolled half the sheeting and left the remaining half under the chair. "Now for the hard part." Holding the side of the chair with both hands, she braced herself and pushed him back to an upright position. "Ugh. You really ought to lose a little weight. Well, there's no time for that now."

She then pushed the chair over again so his right side whumped against the carpet, unrolled the remainder of the sheeting, and again hauled the chair to its upright position.

She again stood back to survey her work. His chair now sat in the middle of a large plastic sheet. "Now for Act Two!" she said. "Tell me something. How do *you* like it when you are at the mercy of someone who never meant you any harm?"

His grunts and weakening struggle against his restraints gave her the answer. "What? Oh, you promise never to do it again? But you've made that promise time and time again, remember? Why should I believe you now? There, you see? No reason at all. So let the games begin. Just a minute," she said, tugging at his shirt. "We can't play games with you fully dressed. You wouldn't be able to feel all the fun things I'm going to do to you. Here, let me help you get naked." She reached into her box and brandished a long pair of pointed scissors.

His eyes opened wide and he screamed against the muffling duct tape.

"You're right. This is no game! If you haven't figured it out yet, this is for real." She smirked at his ghastly complexion. "But don't worry. I'll be careful … sort of."

She cut off as much of his polo shirt as the tape allowed, after which her next target was his trousers. "Aw, were those your new pants?" She threw the pieces into his face. Last, she turned her attention to his boxer shorts. "Oh my, just look at that shrubbery." Clicking her long scissors, she added, "I think I'll have to give you a butch down there." To underline her point she dragged the point along his groin.

In spite of the lethal drug working through his system, his eyes grew wide with terror. Though his muscles were weakening, he struggled as best he could. "Yes, yes," she said, I know you're trying to tell me something—but then, you never listened to me, either. Now you know how frustrating that feels."

Carla reached into her shoebox and arranged a handful of instruments in a row on the table. She held each in turn close to his face to make certain he knew what was in store—the kitchen knife, the stapler, and the cordless drill already loaded with a quarter-inch bit. "There. Think those will be enough to keep you entertained?"

She waved the scissors in a gesture of dismissal. "Not to worry. 'It's just a game,' as you always say." Carla couldn't believe how much she enjoyed her complete control over the monster she'd feared for so many years.

Bending forward in mock surprise, she pointed her tool directly at his groin, and said, "Oh, my, is that a penis I see before me, drooping toward my hand ... 'er ... scissors? Doesn't look at all like the vicious battering ram I've been forced to endure. Perhaps I should cut it off." She clicked the scissors several times under his nose to underscore her remark. "Naw, cutting it off would be too cruel."

A vigorous nod of his head agreed.

"I know ... I'll just snip off the tip." She placed the open scissors around the head and squeezed, savoring his muffled shouts, violent head shakes and squirming body.

"Are you trying to tell me something? I can't understand a word you're saying. Please speak up. Oh-oh, you seem to be making a little puddle down there. Lose control of your bladder, did you? Tsk, tsk. A strong sadistic man like you? How disappointing."

Tears began streaming down his face, dripping onto his bare chest.

"You certainly are making a mess of yourself. Hey! Maybe you're just tired of playing our little bondage games. I'll tell you what. Let's stop the fun and move on to the main event. No, wait! I almost forgot the part you used to like the best." She reached under the table and brandished his aluminum baseball bat. "Remember how you used to like to break my bones and then tell people I fell down the stairs again? Well, turnabout is fair play, as they say."

That said, she swished the bat around her head. "Oops, I missed." Noticing his closed eyes and his head drooping to one side, she said, "Too much excitement? Well, you're in luck." With one hand she grabbed his hair and lifted his head. With the other, she held the bat against his ear. "Yes, you're in luck, sort of. I could never go through with inflicting the pain and humiliation you inflicted on me. Wanna know why? Because if I did, *it would mean I was no better than you.* So I won't need to use these nice toys on your body as planned. Besides, the wine you drank contained enough poison to send six brutes like you on their way to Hell. Before you go, though, I have just one last endearing message: Goodbye and good riddance!"

A weak moan and shake of the head told her the message was received and understood.

Carla let his head droop onto his chest and rolled the bat into a corner. After several deep breaths, she strode to the kitchen and dropped the scissors into the sink she had stoppered earlier. Unscrewing the lid from a can of paint thinner, she poured it over the instrument, hoping the bath would dissolve her fingerprints and sterilize the blades.

On re-entering the dining room, she observed her tormentor hadn't changed position. Moving closer, she detected no sound of breathing. Placing her fingers on his carotid artery and, feeling no pulse, let her breath whoosh into space. "At last!" Moments later she began to whimper. Her hands shook and her breathing morphed into short gasps. Tears flowed freely and her sobs grew louder. Unsteady on her wobbly knees, she staggered to the other end of the table and dropped into a chair, suddenly exhausted.

Emily had warned her of this reaction. "There will be an after-action let-down," she'd said. "You'll probably shake a little and shed some tears of relief."

When the shaking subsided, she reached for her phone and punched in a number. "Emily? It's Carla. It's done and I need your help."

"Is his suitcase packed?"

"It will be by the time you get here."

"We'll be there in an hour. Pour yourself a stiff drink and go pack."

Carla backed her own car out of the garage and parked it on the street, then completed her packing list. By the time Emily's black van drove into the space she'd vacated, Carla had loaded the trunk of her husband's car—a suitcase filled with the clothing and toiletries he usually packed for business trips, plus his golf bag and briefcase.

Carla closed the garage door after Emily killed her engine.

"Gloves," Emily ordered her two companions, donning a pair of surgical gloves as she spoke. She then opened the van's side door. Pointing toward her companions' hair, Emily said, "Call them 'Red' and 'Blackie.' Names won't be necessary. They're part of our special little band of volunteers who help in times like these." She eyed Carla closely. "How are you feeling?"

"I'll be all right."

"Any regrets?"

Carla hesitated before answering, "None ... at least, not yet." Her voice held less determination than before she taped her tormentor to the chair. "But even if I have to spend the rest of my life in jail, I'd do it again just to be rid of the bastard. He was a sadist who didn't deserve to live. I'm *relieved* he's gone, and I can't believe how alive and free I feel."

"I'm glad." To her companions, Emily said, "Hair," and the trio stuffed their tresses into tight-fitting caps. On the command, "Boots," they jammed feet into pairs of new plastic boots. "We're ready."

Carla led her visitors to the dining room. There, her deceased husband lay slumped where his last breath had seeped from mucous-filled nostrils.

At once the black-clad volunteers set to work. They cut the body loose from the chair and rolled it into the plastic sheet along with the bundle of shredded clothing Carla had wrapped separately.

Giving the room a careful scan, Emily pointed to the shoebox. "Those the tools?"

Carla whipped her hands to her face. "Oh, my God. I forgot about the scissors." She scurried to the kitchen to retrieve the scissors and something in which to wrap the shoe box. There! A trash-masher bag from under the sink would be just the thing. A few turns of duct tape and the package was ready to add to the pile.

On the command, "Final check," the three women checked the entire house hunting for overlooked items.

"Is that everything, girls?" Emily asked her cohorts.

"The tape on the chair," Blackie said.

"Good catch." Emily reached into a bag and handed Carla a can of Goo-Gone. "After we leave, remove the tape residue with this."

Final inspection completed, Red and Blackie signaled a "Thumbs up" and dragged the plastic-wrapped body to the garage and stuffed it into Emily's van.

Emily put a hand on Carla's arm. "You've been very brave, my dear. We'll take it from here. Don't forget to report him missing after three days, and be sure to get a copy of the police report. Oh, I almost forgot. Blackie will need your husband's car keys. She'll drive it … someplace."

Carla handed them over, then wrapped her arms around the woman she considered her personal angel. "I don't know how I can ever thank you."

"There *is* one thing you can do, if you're up to it when the time comes."

"*Anything.*"

Emily took Carla's hand and dropped into it a small pendant on a silver chain, identical to the one she wore. "This is the symbol of our little band."

For the first time, Carla noticed the pendant was shaped like a stylized circle of interlocking hands.

"It symbolizes our little group we call 'Helping Hands.' If you accept this, you'll become part of a select, and very secret, sisterhood."

Carla closed her hand around the meaning-filled necklace. "I don't know how I can be useful, but I'll be ready when you call."

"Thank you, my dear. We'll call when another situation needs a helping hand."

"I'll be ready."

Emily kissed her on the cheek to seal the agreement.

"What are you going to do with it—I mean, *him*?"

"Oh, didn't I tell you? When I inherited my husband's mortuary, it came with the cutest little crematory, and ..." she held up a solitary finger, "I can always find room for another deserving customer."

THE THREE-DAY-DEAD
CAT CAPER

▼

Jimmy Briski usually kicked the crumpled beer can just hard enough to send it clattering along the cobblestone street; he liked the way it sounded as it rattled along. This time, though, he wanted to see how far he could make it go, so he kicked it as hard as he could. He gave it a good boot and it sailed off into the air. *That was a good one*, he thought. Trouble was, he hit it with the side of his grungy old sneaker and the can flew all the way into the weed-filled lot next to the abandoned house.

"Oh, fudge," he muttered, and scuffed his way toward the field to retrieve the object of his entertainment. He was pleased with how far the can had traveled, but was annoyed at having to wade through the prickly weeds in his short pants to find it.

When he had picked his way only ten feet into the field, it began to smell like dead cat, and that made him wrinkle his nose. *Pee-yoo! The jinky thing must've been dead at least three days*, he thought, applying his life-long experience with dead-animal smells. That made him look down as he walked; he didn't want to step on any dead cat, especially one that smelled as dead as this one. His mother would have a cow if he went home with stinky shoes.

Just as the rising stench made him slow his step and think about turning back, he noticed a weathered cardboard carton near the rusty oil drum. It had been flattened by the rain and still looked a little soggy, though it hadn't rained for three days now. He shuddered when he remembered playing in that very same refrigerator carton just last week, when it was still new.

Screwing up his courage, he covered his nose and mouth with his not-so-clean hankie and edged closer. He'd seen three-day-dead cats before, but this one smelled different somehow. When he got still closer, he saw why—there was a human hand sticking out from under one end of the cardboard. His heart beat faster, his eyes watered, and his stomach clamored for him to run as fast as he could. But his revulsion was overcome by his curiosity and his feet refused the message to skedaddle.

He reached down and grabbed one corner of the cardboard. He pulled it slowly to one side, hoping the thing wouldn't come apart in his hand. It didn't, but the sudden buzzing from the disturbed swarm of flies made him jump back in alarm. He waved his arms in front of his face until he realized it wasn't *his* flesh they were interested in.

The flies soon returned to their prey, and Jimmy's eyes widened as he stared at the dead woman at his feet. Except for the flies, she was naked. She looked pretty old, too—fifteen or sixteen at least. He noticed the two holes in her chest where the flies gathered, and the bruises around her whizzer. He wanted to shoosh them away, but decided that much intimacy with the corpse might be more than his roiling stomach could handle.

He stared at the dead woman and, hardly breathing, took in the sights from head to toe— he'd never seen a naked woman before, dead or otherwise. After a last look, he turned and ran toward the police station on the next block. It was a relief to get away from the stench.

He bounded up the stone steps of the old brick building to the wide front doors that had "37th Precinct" painted on the frosted glass panels. He pulled at the door. It budged a little, but he wasn't strong or heavy enough to open it far enough to let him in. He rapped on one of the glass panels as hard as he could. Nobody came, so he looked around for something to rap with. There! An old iron doorstop. He picked it up and banged it hard against the wooden part of the door.

That did it. The door opened and a uniformed policeman looked around to see who was battering the station house door.

He didn't see anyone until Jimmy tugged at his pant leg and said, "I'm down here."

The policeman said, "There, now. What do you mean by trying to bash our door in? You want to get arrested for malicious mischief?"

"No, sir," Jimmy said. "I ain't strong enough to open the door by myself and was just trying to get in. I need to talk to the policeman in charge. Quick like!"

The policeman plastered his face with a condescending grin. "Well, now, so you've got business with the man in charge, have you?"

"Yes, I do. Please let me in so I can tell him my big secret and go home. If I'm late for supper I'll have to go to my room without anything to eat, and I'm getting hungry."

"A secret, you say? Well, you can tell it to me, little boy. I'm a genuine policeman," he said, pointing to his badge, "and I can handle whatever is bothering you."

"No, you *can't*," Jimmy said, and kicked the policeman in the shins. "You're too mean."

"Oww," the policeman said, reaching down to rub his bruised leg. "You just assaulted a police officer, you young hoodlum, and for that I'm going to have to take you in to talk to the desk sergeant." He grabbed Jimmy by a shoulder and ushered him into the station.

Jimmy had never been inside a police station before and looked around wide-eyed at all the bustle. In addition to police officers wandering around with holstered guns and nightsticks, he noticed a woman handcuffed to a chair. She was talking to a man in plain clothes whose weathered forefinger poked at a keyboard. Another, with her hands cuffed behind her back, was being led away ... to someplace. Jimmy thought maybe they were taking her out to be hung ... that's what they did in the cowboy movies.

"Hey, Mulroney," hollered a paunchy uniformed officer, "what've you got there, a serial killer?" The laughter that followed got everyone's attention and all eyes turned toward Jimmy. "Caught him stealing a jellybean from old man Winters' candy store, did you?"

Jimmy was humiliated by the fun they were having at his expense. That made him mad, but his anger helped him screw up his courage to take action. He looked around and saw a large gray-haired man with three stripes on his sleeve sitting behind a high desk with a railing in front. "Are you the man in charge?" he sang out. "If you are, I got somethin' to tell you."

"Bring him here, Mulroney," the big man said. "Kid with as much spunk as this tyke deserves a hearing."

Mulroney, now holding Jimmy by his collar, led him to Sergeant O'Malley, the desk sergeant.

"Bring him around here," Sergeant O'Malley said. "I can't see him down there."

Officer Mulroney ushered Jimmy through a battered swinging gate, and deposited him beside the sergeant.

"You can go," Jimmy said to Officer Mulroney, dismissing him in his most authoritative voice. "I need to talk to the sergeant in private."

"So we need to have a private talk, do we?" The sergeant reached out to roll a chair closer for Jimmy to sit on.

"Thanks," Jimmy said, and waited until Mulroney responded to the sergeant's nod of dismissal.

"Now then, what's so important you have to say it in private?"

Jimmy leaned toward the sergeant and whispered, "There's a dead body in the weed field."

"The weed field? Where's that?"

"That's what all the kids call it. It's the field next to the empty house over in the next block."

"A dead body, you say?"

Jimmy nodded.

"And just how do you know it's dead?"

Jimmy looked at the sergeant with a stern face and said, "You'd be dead, too, if you had two holes in your chest and the flies were eating you up."

That revelation made the sergeant take the boy more seriously. "I see. How do you know there are holes in the chest of this ... er ... dead body?"

"Because she's all naked, and the holes are right out there in the open, that's how I know."

"I believe you." The sergeant leaned back in his squeaky chair. "And why do you suppose nobody saw this naked body before now?"

Jimmy was beginning to wonder whether this sergeant had any brains at all. "Because it was covered with a cardboard box and only a hand stuck out ... a little."

Sergeant O'Malley decided this was a matter worth investigating. "Mulroney," he shouted across the hubbub, "get over here." When the officer appeared and saluted, the sergeant pointed at Jimmy and said, "This young man has something to show us. I want you to follow him to the next block, where he will lead you to a naked corpse. Be sure your radio is working, just in case it isn't quite dead yet."

"You pullin' my leg, Sarge?"

"Just do as you're told, Mulroney, and hurry up."

"Yeah," Jimmy said sternly. "If I'm late for supper, I won't get any, and I'll starve to death, and you'll have to bury what's left of my skeleton."

"That should convince you that a bit of urgency is in order," said the sergeant. "Now git!"

Grumbling, Mulroney followed Jimmy to the weed field, where he quickly smelled the stench of death. When he did, his respect for the credibility of his guide rose several notches.

"Okay, now watch your step," Jimmy admonished. "Don't step over there," he said, pointing to a space close to the old rusty oil drum.

"And why not?" Mulroney asked.

"Because," Jimmy said, "you shouldn't mess with the evidence."

"Evidence, is it?"

"Uh-huh. There's a man's footprint over there that wasn't there four days ago. If you step on it, you'll ruin it."

"And may I ask how you know when this footprint was made?"

Jimmy wondered how it was this officer didn't know anything about police work. "Because my pals and I were playing here four days ago and the footprint wasn't here."

"I see. Then how come the body here—"

"Look, now I'm late for supper and I'm gonna get it for something that ain't my fault." He started making his way toward the street.

"Hold on a minute." Mulroney called the station on his shoulder radio and asked for the desk sergeant. "Sarge? Mulroney here. We're standing at the side of a corpse, just as this young man said. "It's—"

"It's been dead three days," Jimmy chimed in.

"Yeah," Mulroney echoed. "It's been dead three days. Better get a crime scene team here right away. We'll wait until they arrive."

"I'll be damned," the sergeant said. "Look. When they get there, bring the boy back here for a few minutes. Tell him we'll make it okay with his parents about his being late."

"Ten-four." To Jimmy, he said, "You heard that okay, did you?"

"Yeah. Wait. Shouldn't we cover the body, or something?"

Mulroney's respect for the boy took another notch upward. "We should at that, but the crime lab bus will be here in a few minutes and they'll take over."

Ten minutes later the van arrived. Jimmy "briefed" the team as they cordoned off the area with yellow tape. After he showed them all the places they shouldn't step, he and Officer Mulroney headed back to the station.

"Well, now," Sergeant O'Malley said, beaming, "It seems we have a fine young detective here, and we should apologize for doubting his word." To Jimmy, he said, "But you must admit, young man, it seemed a little strange that after seeing a naked dead body you didn't go screaming home to your mother."

"That wouldn't be right," Jimmy said. "When you find a body as dead as this one, you're supposed to tell the police."

"You watch a lot of television, Jimmy?"

"Some. But I read detective stories, too."

"Good. Now here's the deal. You've got a good head on your shoulders, and a pretty good eye for clues. So before we do anything else, we're going to make you an official junior detective so you can help us out with this crime. That okay with you?"

Jimmy puffed out his chest and said, "Ten-four."

"Now then, to fix it so you can get under the crime scene tape, you'll need an I.D. badge." He reached into his top drawer and took out an empty badge holder. "Marge," he called to a passing policewoman, "take this young man down to booking and have them whomp up a photo I.D. for him. We need it quick, like yesterday."

The policewoman didn't understand what was going down, but knew enough to do as she was told. Taking Jimmy by the hand, she led him downstairs to the booking area, where she had his picture taken.

The photographer cropped the picture, typed Jimmy's full name along its bottom edge, then slid it into the I.D. holder. The policewoman adjusted the length of the lanyard so the I.D. holder would reach to Jimmy's chest rather than his knees.

When the policewoman presented the grinning boy to the sergeant, Sgt. O'Malley smiled and said, "That's better. Now everybody will know you belong at the crime scene. But first, you and I and Officer Mulroney are going to report in to your parents so they'll know why you're late for supper. Soon as we do that I'll be sending you right back to the crime scene to give 'em a hand. If that's okay with you, that is."

"Sure thing," Jimmy said, saluting. "Can you *really* fix it so I won't end up in the cooler? My Mom'll be chewing nails by now."

"Don't worry. We'll fix it, all right, and then take you out for a nice, juicy hamburger before sending you back to work."

Sergeant O'Malley assigned a replacement to handle the desk, then led Jimmy and Mulroney to a squad car. He pointed Jimmy to the front seat. "Try not to touch anything, okay?"

"Can we play the siren when we get to my house?"

"Well, maybe just a little squirt. We don't want the neighbors to wet their pants now, do we?"

When they arrived at Jimmy's house with the siren growling, his mother was already on the front porch, obviously worried about her missing little boy. Her hands flew to her mouth when Jimmy stepped out of the patrol car, then grabbed him in a bear-hug when he reached the porch. "Where have you been ... and what have you done *now*?" she demanded, after assuring herself her little boy was unhurt. "Have you been arrested for something?"

"Now, now, Missus Briski," the sergeant said, "he hasn't done anything wrong. As a matter of fact, he did something very brave, and that's why he's late for dinner. He would have been home earlier, but we needed his help with a very important matter."

Jimmy's father now stood next to his wife and heard the last words. "What are you talking about?" he said.

"Well, now," the sergeant said, "if you will notice, Jimmy here is helping us with a police matter, and he's wearing his official police I.D. badge to prove it." He pointed to the boy's chest.

Jimmy stuck out his torso so everyone could get a better look.

"If you folks don't mind," the sergeant said, "I'll let Jimmy tell you all about it later. Right now, we gotta get him something to eat and rush back to the crime scene before it gets dark. C'mon, Jimmy." As the trio headed for the patrol car, he threw over his shoulder, "We'll take good care of him and have him back a little after dark."

They climbed into the car and drove off with the siren wailing and the light bar flashing.

Jimmy waved and grinned at the gaping neighbors rubber-necking on the sidewalk as the car rolled by.

Arriving at the crime scene after gobbling a hamburger and milk shake on the way, Jimmy scampered from the car and ran toward the people tromping around the weed-filled lot.

Waving his arms, he shouted, "Not there, not there! Don't step there!"

Having been briefed about the young crime-fighting wizard, everyone froze in position until Jimmy told them—again—where they could, and could not, step. "Don't step near the rusty oil drum," he said, "'specially around the back side. And don't walk on this path over here," he said, pointing. "It's got the killer's footprint on it." He showed them three other places to avoid, and two people were dispatched to surround them all with yellow tape.

When Jimmy was done hollering directions, one of the crime scene people squatted beside him and said, "Hi. I'm Detective Drum. Call me John, okay?"

Jimmy stuck out his hand—he'd never shaken hands with a real live detective before, but thought this John guy didn't look at all like the detectives in his comic books. He was a little too short and his jaw wasn't square enough.

"How old are you, Jimmy?" the detective asked.

"Seven ... and a half," Jimmy said. "I'm gonna be eight, you know."

Being a detective, Drum thought he could have deduced that fact all by himself. "You're getting to be a ripe old age, aren't you? So how about telling us what you know about the deceased."

"The who?"

"The dead woman."

"Oh." Jimmy pulled himself up and told the detective about finding the body and about the holes in her chest. "And she was beat up some before he killed her, too," he added.

"What do you mean?"

"She was naked, you know, and I saw some black marks around her whizzer."

"Her ... oh, right." Drum made a mental note to have a rape kit run. "You really are an observant lad. Anything else?"

"Yeah. She wasn't killed there."

"How can you tell?"

"Me and my buddies play in this field a lot and we pretty much know where all the paths are. The body made a new path when somebody dragged it there."

"Good man. We already found the drag marks. Looks like it was dragged from that house over there."

"Yeah. I ain't sure, but I bet you'll find some footprints over by that basement window." He pointed toward the abandoned house.

"We'll get somebody right on it," the detective said. Changing the subject, he added, "I believe you told Officer Mulroney the body's been dead three days."

"Yep."

"How do you know that?"

"Heck, that's easy. We was playing here four days ago and there wasn't any dead body here then. But it was there today when I kicked the can here and it smelled like a three-day-dead cat."

"The body?"

"Yeah. So it must'a been put there pretty soon after the rain stopped—that's why we stopped playing and ran home. Besides, it was getting a little dark."

"So you figure the body was dragged over there shortly after that, right?"

"Yeah. It'd take that long for the stink to get as bad as a three-day-dead cat."

Detective Drum was amused by Jimmie's unit of measurement. "Good thinking," he said, chuckling as he added, "I think the medical examiner is going to start measuring time-of-death by cat-stink. Now tell me about that footprint on the path."

"Okay, c'mon over here, but don't step on the path. There might be other stuff to find." He led the detective to the footprint.

"Y'see that?" he said, pointing.

"Yes, I see it."

"Well, it wasn't there when we played here four days ago, like I said."

"How can you tell?" By now the detective hung on every word uttered by his young guide.

"When we play Cowboys 'n' Indians, we sometimes make signs on the trails—the paths. If you stoop down and look at this footprint from here," Jimmy squatted to demonstrate, "you can still see what's left of the arrow I made in the dirt with my stick, right smack dab in the middle of where that footprint is now."

"That means someone stepped on your arrow, right?"

"Sure does."

"I think I get it," the detective said. "You stopped playing because it started to rain, so the footprint must have been made after the rain stopped, but soon enough to give the corpse time to smell like a three-day-dead cat."

"Yeah. Three days ago. That's when the cat ... the body ... musta been killed."

Detective Drum smiled at the wisdom of the seven-and-a-half-year-old boy. "Just two more things, Jimmy. You said we shouldn't disturb the area around that rusty oil drum. Can you tell me about that?"

"Sure. The old drum is a good hiding place, so maybe there's more stuff to find around there. I'd look real close."

"We will, I promise. Uh ... I don't suppose you'd have any idea who did this?"

"*Sure*, I do."

"You do?" The surprise on the detective's face made his bushy eyebrows leap toward the top of his head.

"What? You think I'm lying?" Jimmy stuck out his lower lip.

"No, no. It's just that you surprised me. Who do you think committed this crime?"

"Fat Freddy, that's who! That old guy—he's gotta be seventeen, at least—who lives in the empty house." Jimmy again pointed to the house on the edge of the weed field.

"Why do you think Fat Freddy killed this woman?"

"He likes to show off by waving a big ole' rusty gun he's got. Says he's gonna shoot us all if we don't stop throwin' rocks at the house. But we never believe him because he never showed us no bullets."

"I see. So you think he's got some bullets someplace and shot the girl with them."

"Yeah. Musta. She prob'ly freaked when he took his pants down. He's always tryin' to show girls his whizzer. I bet he got mad and shot her before she could run away."

"I think we'd better have a talk with Fat Freddy." The detective took a cell phone from his pocket and punched in a number. "Lieutenant? Drum. We've got a suspect for the empty-lot murder over here ... yeah, they're still processing the scene,

Sarge, but I think we'll need the SWAT team to take him down—the suspect's got a gun—"

"*Wait!*" Jimmy said, tugging at the detective's pant leg.

"Hold on, Loo," Drum said into the phone.

"I can get him to come out without no SWAT team," Jimmy said. "That'd just scare him off."

The detective spoke into his phone. "I'll call you right back." He broke the connection and squatted beside Jimmy. "You got a better idea?"

"I think so." He pointed toward the processing team. "You get those guys to raise a little rumpus so Fat Freddy will peek out the side window there. You hide a couple guys around the front porch and I'll get him to come out. Then you arrest him."

"What about his gun?"

"Don't worry about it. He waves it around inside, but he'd be too scared to take it out of the house."

Drum wasn't sure about the logic of that statement, but said, "Okay, sounds good." He told his Lieutenant he wouldn't be needing the SWAT team because Jimmy was going to take the perp down single-handed. When the Lieutenant asked him what the hell he was talking about, he just chuckled and hung up.

Drum sprinted to where the scene was being processed, and said, "Listen up. We're going to arrest a suspect over in that house and we need you to make a diversion so we can get him to come out." He told them what to do when he gave the signal, and went back to where Jimmy was standing.

Jimmy said, "Okay, now you and your partner hunker down beside the porch steps and you can grab him when he comes out."

The detective waved the signal and squatted beside the porch stairs, with a patrol officer similarly positioned on the other side.

When they saw the signal, the crime scene team began jumping up and down like Indians around a campfire, whooping and hollering and waving their arms.

That was Jimmy's cue to pick up three rocks the size of golf balls and hurl one at the front door of the house, hollering, "HEY, FAT-ASS! C'MON OUT! WE WANNA SEE YOUR FAMOUS SHRIVELED WHIZZER." When there was no immediate response from inside, he battered the door with another rock and shouted, "HEY, LARD-BUTT! YOUR MOTHER EATS HORSE-BISCUITS!"

That did it. The front door burst open and Fat Freddy lumbered out shouting, "I'll get you for that, you snotty sonuvabitch. I'll wring your skinny neck until your eyes pop out!"

He jogged across the porch and bounded down the eight steps two at a time. He was only three feet behind Jimmy when his foot reached the sidewalk at the bottom of the steps.

At that instant, the two officers jumped up, showed their badges with one hand, and pointed their pistols at the red-faced suspect with the other.

"Stop! Police! Put your hands on top of your head."

Detective Drum was relieved there was no sign of a gun, rusty or otherwise.

Freddy froze, put his hands high in the air, and wet his pants.

By the time his hands were handcuffed behind his back, Freddy began crying and tried to wipe his tears on his shoulders.

Detective Drum told the officer to Mirandize their suspect and take him to the police station for questioning.

It was only after Jimmy calmed down from the excitement of the capture that he noticed a television camera pointed in his direction.

Later, when the police car—siren growling and red lights flashing—pulled to the curb in front of his house, Jimmy leaped out and ran inside to tell his parents the story of what he called 'The Big Takedown.' After narrating the details of his exciting day more than twice—especially the part about Freddy confessing to the murder

R. F. Mager

and the rape on the way to the police station—he went upstairs to brush his teeth and put on his pajamas.

Then, with his I.D. badge around his neck and his eyelids at half mast, he settled onto the living room couch between his Mom and Dad to watch himself on the ten o'clock news.

Mysterious Ways

▼

He pulled the folds of his tattered overcoat closer, hoping the threadbare cloth would help shut out the winter cold. Trudging along the street with feet held apart to keep from slipping on the icy sidewalks, the old man was determined to arrive at the church before the rehearsal ended. It was a dreary, sub-zero day, but he knew the beautiful choral music would warm his tired soul.

An icy gust told him it was too cold to stand in his usual listening place under the stained glass windows. He would freeze solid, if he tried. The wind continued to push him along until he found himself standing at the foot of the church stairs. *Well,* he thought, *if you think I should . . .* Lifting one foot, then another, he climbed the stone risers and faced the heavy doors. He worried about touching the icy brass handle. His hand might stick to it.

Pulling a soiled handkerchief from his pocket, he wrapped it around the uninviting surface. Using all his strength, he managed to open the door just far enough to slip inside.

He rubbed his hands together as he shivered just inside the door. The warmth felt, oh, so good. And the choir—he'd never heard their music from *inside* until this freezing day. He looked up at the windows and envied the saints depicted in the stained glass—*they* got to hear the music from the comfort of the sanctuary every day. As he stood rubbing the cold from his hands, he swayed and let his eyelids droop while the wondrous notes seeped into his pores and into his heart.

"May I help you?"

He opened his eyes to see a matronly woman standing in front of him. "Please," he said. "I just want to listen to the music."

"This is a closed rehearsal, so I'm afraid I'm going to have to ask you to leave."

"But it's so cold outside, I thought you might allow me—just this once—to hear it from the inside. Please, ma'am, if you'll just let me sit in the back I won't be any trouble at all. It's just that your music warms my soul. I *must* hear it."

"I'm sorry, but spectators are not allowed."

"Would it hurt to let an old man enjoy the glorious sounds of your voices? Just this once I'd like to be able to listen from inside the church."

"Inside? I don't understand."

"Usually, I stand outside in the bushes under the windows to listen. But it's so cold today I thought you might allow me just this once to hear it from inside."

"Wait here," she said, and strode off to consult with the choir director. He watched as they conversed, knowing they were deciding his fate. The bearded man with the baton looked in his direction as the woman pointed. When she returned, she said, "All right. You can sit in that armchair behind the last pew and listen."

"Oh, thank you, thank you," the man replied. Sinking into the comfortable chair, he cupped his hands around his ears to let every note penetrate his faded hearing. He smiled when he heard the sweet voice of the soloist. Rather than the piercing tones of some choirs' sopranos, *this* voice sounded as if each velvet note were wrapped in the wings of an angel and delivered with love ... just for him.

When the rehearsal was over, the musicians collected their music and chatted among themselves.

"Have you noticed?" the stern woman said to the choir director. "That man we let in hasn't moved since the singing stopped. He just sits there motionless with that smile on his face."

Together, the two walked slowly up the aisle. Still the man didn't move. "Excuse me," the director said, "but we're finished and have to lock up the church now."

The man remained motionless.

"If you ask me," the woman said, "I think he's dead."

"Dead?" The director moved closer and looked into the open eyes of the old man. Gently, he put his fingers on the wrinkled neck to check for a pulse. "Yes, I believe you're right. But his eyes are open and the smile is still on his face. He must have died when the music stopped."

The stern woman felt a tear slide down her cheek. "Now I wish I hadn't been so brusque with him. He seemed like a nice man. Do you know who he is?"

"No, I don't believe I've ever seen him before."

"Should we call the police?" she asked. "We'll have to have him removed before we can lock up."

"I'll do it." Consulting his pocket phone list, the director punched the number of the local Constabulary.

Less than ten minutes later, the door opened and a familiar policeman entered. "Good morning, George," he said. "I hear you have a problem."

"Yes, and I'm glad they sent *you*," the choir director replied. "We allowed a homeless person to audit our rehearsal and he apparently died while listening to us sing. There he is, still smiling."

"Homeless person?" the policeman said. He sidled along the aisle for a closer look. "Why, don't you know who he is?"

"No."

"Remember all the large donations you received when the choir was about to go under because contributions were so scarce?"

"Yes, of course. We never did find out where they came from."

The policeman nodded in the direction of corpse. "That's *him*."

"Who? You mean—?"

"Yes, *A. Nonymouse* himself."

The remaining singers gasped and murmured their surprise.

"I ran him in a few times for urinating in the bushes out there under the stained-glass window, but stopped rousting him when I learned he was harmless and only interested in listening to your music. I even stopped and listened with him now and then, and sometimes we talked. Your sounds brought tears to his eyes, you know. Sometimes, his hands moved as though he were conducting. Occasionally, he sort of sang along as well. After a while I got the impression he knew every word to each song you performed. Which reminds me. You know that cantata you've been rehearsing?"

"The one by A. Nonymouse?"

"Yes," the policeman said, smiling. "I guess you never made the connection between—"

"My God! *He* wrote it?"

The policeman nodded. "And many others. He told me all about them. It's funny, you know. He never talked about himself—only about his music. You can tell by his smile you performed a gigantic kindness by letting him hear his music from inside a warm room. I'll always be grateful to you for that."

As the policeman called for a hearse, the remaining choir members slowly gathered around the body. Then, as if directed by an angel, they began to sing *Nearer My God to Thee*.

When they lifted the body, an over-stuffed envelope fell from an inside pocket, spilling a shower of hundred-dollar bills onto the floor. On the envelope was written, "To the Main Street Church ... Thank you, and may God bless you all."

It was signed, *A. Nonymouse*.

WHO'S THE DUMMY?

▼

The District Attorney jabbed a finger toward his scowling Assistant DA. "I don't give a hoot-owl's toot what *you* want," he said. "We're short-handed, and the least you can do is pull up your socks and fill in, short notice or no."

"But—"

"Look, Blorkman, I don't have time for your whining. I know there's an election coming up and you're itching to sit in my chair. But you're not the DA yet, so snap on your jockstrap and start pulling your weight—of which there is an ample supply, I might add."

Blorkman heaved his bulk to a near-vertical position. "But the trial begins today. I won't have time to prepare, and—"

"You wouldn't have time if the trial were six *months* from today — unless, of course, you quit

153

wasting everybody's time with those incessant practical jokes of yours."

"But I—"

"Knock it off, Blorkman. You're not making any friends with your demented jokes, you know. I suppose you know I had to take a lot of heat because you glued the bailiff's ass to his chair last week. The judge was really steamed over that. She still hasn't gotten over your gluing her gavel to the bench—"

"But it was only a—"

"And stuffing chewing gum into the sandwich machine's coin slot and—"

"But—"

"Cutting a hole in the backside of the judge's robe."

"But those were just innocent pranks—"

"But nothing. You've made a lot of enemies with those pranks. Now, get serious about this case. The legwork's already been done, so get the folders from the clerk, pick up the police and coroner's reports, and give 'em a once over. It oughta be a slam-dunk for a big-time ADA like you." The district attorney grinned as the ADA turned to leave. *This is gonna be good*, he thought, rubbing his hands together as a mischievous grin spread across his face.

Blam! Blam! Blam! The judge whacked her gavel so hard the head flew off the handle, landed on the floor, and rolled to the feet of the bailiff. Picking it up, he handed it back to the judge with a wink. "I believe this is yours, Your Honor."

Reassembling the gavel as best she could, she bellowed, "Order in the court!" It was a vain attempt to quell the hubbub erupting at the prosecutor's objection.

"I object!" the prosecutor wailed again. "I object most strenuously."

"I can *see* that," the judge said, "but what are you objecting *to*, Mr. Blorkman?"

"The outrageous behavior of the defense counsel, that's what. Defense is trying to put a damned dum—sorry, Your Honor—a *dummy* on the stand." He waved his arms in futility.

"What's wrong with *that*?" The judge raised her eyebrows in feigned innocence, clearly enjoying this twist to her otherwise hum-drum day. Having eagerly joined the plot to turn the tables on the pompous jokester, she found the giggles and elbow-jabs of the spectators only added to her barely-concealed delight.

The prosecutor continued his rant. "Defense is trying to make a mockery of this court! Why, the very notion of putting a block of wood on the stand is ludicrous to the extreme. Besides, asking a dummy to testify is the same as asking the *defendant* to testify."

"Sit *down*, Mr. Blorkman. Unless the rules have been changed since yesterday, the accused is entitled to call witnesses in his defense. Is that not true?"

"Of course, Your Honor. But—but a *dummy*? Why, it's not even alive—"

The defense attorney leaped to his feet. "The puppet is as alive as its operator makes it, Your Honor, but the puppet and its operator are *not* one and the same."

"They're not?"

"No, Your Honor. The whole *point* of the ventriloquial art is to create a puppet that is a distinctly different person from its operator."

Looking at Blorkman, the judge spread her hands. "See?"

"But Your Honor. The defendant is accused of killing and dismembering one Ronnie Chitlin, a mere ten-year-old boy. Surely the court has an obligation to take this case seriously. Putting a dummy on the stand—"

"I say again, Blorkman, sit *down!* I have not yet ruled on your objection. Until then, please shut up." She turned again to the defense counsel. "Now then, Mr. Sterling, tell the court why you think I should allow a dummy—"

"*Puppet*, Your Honor."

"What's the difference?"

"If you call them dummies, they find ways to get even."

"I see." Her expression made it clear she didn't see at all. "Are you mocking this court, young man?"

"Not at all, Your Honor. It's just that the puppets, or figures, are insulted by being called 'dummies,' and find ways to even the score with their operators."

"By 'operators,' I take it you mean ventriloquists?"

"Yes, Your Honor. Insulted puppets may decide to sulk in the middle of a performance, or pretend to forget their lines, or something even more embarrassing."

"All right, we'll refer to them as puppets. Now tell me why you want to put a puppet on the stand."

"The puppet is an eyewitness to the event, Your Honor."

"But how can the puppet testify? It isn't even human, much less alive."

"But that's the point, Your Honor. The goal of the ventriloquist is to become skillful enough to give life to his little friend. I'll be glad to call an expert witness to explain the basics."

"I think that would be a good idea, Mr. Sterling."

"I call Mr. Nicolas Pellow to the stand."

A slightly-built man with a twinkle in his eyes and a receding hairline rose from the benches and came forward to be sworn. Placing a worn fiberboard suitcase at his feet, he raised his right hand.

The bailiff strode forward, thrust his Bible at the witness and recited his truth-mantra like an auctioneer peddling a pig in a poke.

"I do," said Pellow.

"I do, too," echoed a muffled voice from the suitcase.

"What was that?" the judge asked.

The bailiff glanced at the judge, then retreated to his courtroom perch.

"That was Perky, Your Honor," Pellow said, pointing to the suitcase. "I brought a puppet in case I'm asked to demonstrate a point."

"Uh-huh," the judge said, hiding a grin behind a cupped hand. "Carry on, Mr. Sterling."

Sterling strode forward to qualify the witness as an expert. "How long have you been a performing ventriloquist?"

"Since I was nine years old. I began performing for family and friends, then did gigs in schools and worked my way up to bars and nightclubs."

"Don't believe him!" the muffled voice shouted from the suitcase. "*I'm* the ventriloquist here. Let me *outa* here!"

Pellow thumped the suitcase with a foot.

"Can't you control that thing any better than that?" the judge asked.

"It's not easy, Your Honor. He has a mind of his own."

At that, the prosecutor rose and spread his hands. In his best whiney voice, he pleaded, "I say again, Your Honor, defense is making a mockery of this court."

"Blickery blockery, Blorkman's a mockery!" It was the muffled voice from the suitcase.

The witness whacked the suitcase with an open palm.

"Mr. Pellow, either you control that thing or I will hold it in contempt." *Good God*, the judge thought, *I'm talking about an invisible dummy as though it were alive. I didn't think I could do that, but here I am—and not even trying.* Red-faced, she added, "Please move on, Mr. Sterling."

"Thank you, Your Honor. I'd like to ask all the ventriloquists in the audience to stand."

Twelve men, five women, two small boys, and a girl stood, working hard to arrange their faces into serious expressions.

"How many of you have watched Mr. Pellow perform professionally?" Sterling asked.

All the hands shot up.

"How many consider him a superb ventriloquist?"

Again, all hands were raised.

"How many of you consult him for advice on figure-making and the art of ventriloquism?"

Hands punctured the air yet again.

"Thank you. You may sit down," Sterling said. To the witness, he said, "Have you ever won any awards for your ventriloquial skills?"

Pellow listed several awards and trophies earned at conventions for performing ventriloquists and magicians.

Blorkman waved a casual hand in the direction of the witness. "The prosecution stipulates the witness is a qualified expert. Now, please, may we proceed with this farce?"

Sterling acknowledged the distraught prosecutor with a bow, then turned to the witness. "Mr. Pellow, you are being asked to testify on the issue of whether the puppet and ventriloquist are one and the same."

"I think the best way to answer that is to let me take Perky out of his suitcase and—"

"It's about time, you moron," the muffled voice shouted.

Pellow lifted the case to his lap and lifted the lid. A ghoulish head appeared over the rim. It wore a gaunt greenish face and matted hair, and rotted teeth protruded in every direction. One eye dangled from its socket on a single sinew.

"This is Perky," ventured the mild-mannered ventriloquist. "He's a zombie, recently dug up."

As Perky's good eye scanned the room, the dangling eyeball swung to and fro with every move of the head. The puppet's constant motion made it impossible for the viewers to take their eyes from it. Pellow, on the other hand, sat motionless and without expression, giving the audience no reason to look at him. He was, in effect, invisible.

"Your Honor!" the prosecutor shouted.

"Sit down, Mr. Blorkman. Mr. Sterling, I confess I see very little resemblance between the puppet and the ventriloquist."

"Exactly the point, Your Honor," Sterling said. "Mr. Pellow is so skilled there is no way Perky can be mistaken for anyone other than himself. The instant Mr. Pellow picks up the puppet, it becomes Perky, the zombie."

"Is that true, Mr. Pellow?" the judge asked.

"Yes, Your Honor. Once the puppet comes to life, it can only behave in character. There's no way I can make him respond in any other way."

"Thank you. Questions, Mr. Blorkman?"

A defeated Blorkman lumbered to his feet, mumbling as he approached the witness.

"He really *is* fat, ain't he?" Perky asked his operator, the loose eyeball drawing titters with each dangle.

Pellow instantly put a hand over Perky's mouth. "Stop that!"

"There," triumphed Blorkman, looking and pointing squarely at Pellow. "YOU said that, didn't you?"

"I only said, 'Stop that'."

"I mean the other thing."

"No, I would never insult an officer of the court."

Blorkman shook his head in resignation. "No further questions."

"In that case," the judge offered, "let me hear evidence on the motion."

"If I may, Your Honor," Sterling said, "I'm ready to support the motion to allow my client's puppet to testify."

"The court will listen with interest," the judge said.

"While preparing for this case," Sterling began, "I found seven legal precedents for allowing a witness with a split personality to testify." He summarized three of the cases in which judges ruled it permissible for someone with several personalities to testify either against the others, or against the owner of the primary personality. "I believe this case falls within the scope of those precedents. This is a capital case, so we must explore every avenue that may shed light on the truth of this serious matter." *That's a load of bullbleep, but if it will help give Blorkman a dose of his own medicine ...*

The spectators leaned forward on their benches.

The judge frowned. "In view of these precedents, I will allow the defendant's puppet, Mr. Sniffy O'Malley, to testify, but—"

The spectators applauded

Blorkman leaped to his feet to object. "This is a caricature of justice, Your Honor. I demand a mistrial."

"We haven't *had* a trial yet, Mr. Blorkman. Be patient and you may get your wish. For now, just sit down. Mr. Pellow, you are excused."

"What about *me*?" the zombie shouted.

"There's no excuse for you—you step down, too."

Sterling rose and approached the witness box. "Thank you, Your Honor. The defendant's puppet is on the prosecution's witness list, so his presence can't be a surprise to Mr. Blorkman. If he had objections, he should have voiced them before the trial began. I now call Mr. Sniffy O'Malley to the stand."

The judge waggled her pen at the defense attorney. "Let there be no mistake, Mr. Sterling. The *puppet* is being called as the witness, *not* the defendant. The minute the defendant utters a word on his own behalf, I'll hold you in contempt. Is that clear?"

"Yes, Your Honor." Sterling repeated, "I call Mr. Sniffy O'Malley to the stand."

The defendant reached into the suitcase by his side and removed a puppet. Built to resemble an old man, it sported a head of grizzled white hair above a craggy face. The bright green trousers and red-and-white checkered coat seemed a perfect costume for an aging circus barker. As soon as the defendant's left hand grabbed the control stick in the puppet's back, the figure came to life. Every tug on the controls and the smallest movement of the head changed the facial expression from surprise, to sadness, to pleasure.

As the defendant made his way to the witness stand, the puppet acknowledged the spectators with a slight nod, a grin, and a wink. Once settled, the defendant placed the puppet on his left knee.

"Get your hand out of there," O'Malley rasped, scowling. "Can't you do that without groping?"

The defendant rolled his eyes, but said nothing.

"Bailiff, swear in the witness."

The bailiff picked up his tattered Bible and approached the witness. Exactly four feet from the witness stand, he froze, as if suddenly struck by the absurdity of what he was being asked to do. He looked plaintively at the judge.

"Which one, Your Honor?"

"The little one. Now, get on with it."

Feeling more foolish than he ever had, but relishing the moment, the bailiff approached the puppet. "Raise your right hand."

When the puppet's right arm shot into the air, the "astonished" bailiff stumbled backward and dropped his Bible.

Laughter erupted.

Pretending to regain his composure with some difficulty, he retrieved his book and held it at arm's length toward the puppet.

The puppet leaned forward, sneered, and said, "You buy that tie at a flea market? If I had to wear a tie like that I'd slash my wrists and bleed to death."

Further discombobulated by the sassy puppet, the "flustered" bailiff tried to continue. "Er ... do you swear to tell the truth, the whole truth, and nothing but the truth, so help you God?" While delivering this well-rehearsed speech, the bailiff wondered how idiotic this would look on the six o'clock news.

"I diddly do," Sniffy responded.

"State your name and occupation for the record."

"My name is Sniffy O'Malley, and I am employed as a comedian by this imposter." He tossed his head in the direction of the "vent" on whose knee he sat.

Audience titters drew another whack of the gavel.

The relieved bailiff returned to his post, mumbling about the idiotic things he was expected to do to keep his job.

The defense attorney rose and approached the witness. "Mr. O'Malley, you've sworn to tell the truth. Are you familiar with the defendant?"

"Not as familiar as he gets with me. He's got a cold hand wrapped around my spine as we speak."

"Can you remember where you were on the night of September seventeenth?"

"Sure."

"Well?"

"Well, what?"

"Where were you?"

"Oh. I spent the evening sitting on the workbench of Mister Bumblefingers here." The puppet jerked his head toward the defendant.

"And what was the defendant doing during that time?"

"Fumbling around with the ... uh ... mechanism of Titsie Turner."

"*Exactly* what was he doing?"

"One of her eyelashes fell off during a performance and he was trying to glue it back on."

"Was that all?"

"No. One of her—you know—had slipped out of her dress and looked a little droopy, so he gave her a little uplift and glued the thing back in."

"Uplift?"

"Sure. We don't call her Va-Va for nothing, you know."

"Va-Va?"

"Yeah. Va-va-voom! She's really stacked."

The defense attorney waited patiently until the spectators recovered their decorum. "I see. Did you know Ronnie Chitlin, the deceased?"

"Absolutely. A great kid."

"And did you see him during the night in question?"

"Of course. I saw the whole thing."

"Now consider this question carefully," the defense attorney continued. "Did you see the defendant murder Ronnie Chitlin?"

O'Malley paused to let the tension mount. "Are you for real? Mister Lip-flapper here can be a little grouchy, but he definitely is not capable of such a cowardly act."

Mr. Sterling stood tall, formed his face into a satisfied grin, and bowed to the prosecutor. "Your witness."

Blorkman shook his head in resignation. "Oh, all right." Hauling his bulk from the chair, he spoke first to the judge. "But I want my objection to this melodrama on the record."

"So noted," the judge said. "Now please proceed."

Approaching the witness stand, Blorkman addressed the defendant. "Are you a self-taught ventriloquist?"

The defendant sat mute and motionless as O'Malley shot his head back and laughed. "Nice try, Fatso, but you're gonna go to jail if you keep that up."

Blorkman turned to the judge for help.

"Sorry, Blorkman. You stepped into that one all by yourself. Now move along."

Somewhat chastened, the prosecutor turned to the puppet. "You testified that you saw Ronnie Chitlin the night of the murder. Is that true?"

"Would I lie?"

"Was he still alive when you saw him?"

"You bet."

"And did you see the defendant there at the same time?"

"Of course."

"And just what was the defendant doing?"

"I just told you. He was rebuilding Titsie Turner's boobs."

"And after that?

"He began dismembering Ronnie."

"Aha! *Dismembering* him! You mean after he killed him?"

"No."

"You're telling this court that the defendant dismembered the deceased while he was still *alive*?"

"Yeah."

"So you *are* an eyewitness to the gruesome murder?"

"Whoa, there, Tubby. I didn't say anything about a murder."

"But you just said—"

"I said Ronnie was dismembered while he was still alive. I didn't say he was murdered." The puppet adopted a mischievous grin. "This guy," he said, tossing his head in the direction of the defendant, "was very gentle with him."

The prosecutor again turned to the judge for help.

"Sorry, Blorkman. *You're* asking the questions."

"Oh, all right. If the deceased was dismembered, and he wasn't murdered, how did he get dead?"

"I didn't say he got dead. I said he got dismembered—not dead."

"And that's possible because—?"

Pausing for effect, O'Malley said, "Because Ronnie was being rebuilt, reconditioned, and otherwise spruced up for a big show."

Suddenly seeing the light, Blorkman shouted, "Wait a minute. Wait just a minute! Are you telling this court that Ronnie Chitlin was—is—a *puppet?*" He shook his head as if to clear cobwebs from his brain.

The spectators erupted in laughter, joined by the bailiff and the judge.

When at last the spectators quieted, the judge rose and spoke in a sonorous tone. "The prosecution has been unable, or unwilling, to produce evidence proving that the alleged decedent is, in fact, dead—or even slightly injured. He has failed to produce a suitable corpse, and therefore failed to prove a crime was even committed. I see no other course but to dismiss this case."

When the applause at last diminished, she continued. "And you, Mr. Blorkman, owe a large debt of gratitude to these people who worked long hours to teach you a lesson you seem in serious need of learning."

Blorkman slumped in his chair like a deflating balloon and banged his head against the table, just as a barrage of camera flashes emanating from reporters and audience filled the air.

The snickering reporters rushed from the courtroom, eager to make their afternoon deadline.

Standing with arms spread wide, the grinning judge intoned, "Court is adjourned."

Life is Sweet

▼

I live—if you can call it that—in a little shack along the edge of Black Creek. I don't know why they call it that. It doesn't look any different from White Creek, over there on the other side of the railroad tracks. But I'm not complaining. The water's clean, and sometimes gives up a fish or two. Not enough to live on, but it helps, and fishin' gives me something to do.

My shack is just right for an old bachelor—no cracks in the walls, the roof is tight, and I got running water and a fireplace. Plenty of firewood to chop, too, though the choppin' part is hard when you've only got one arthritic leg and a crutch.

But I'm not complaining. Every once in a while I hobble down to the crossroads to buy a few necessaries. Sometimes I stop in at the saloon, just to be sociable with some of my neighbors and catch up on the goings-on, you understand.

For excitement, I sometimes take my bucket to scavenge along the railroad tracks for pieces of coal flung off a passing coal car. You might say it ain't much of a life, but let me tell you something: I'm getting a lot more out of life than those poor guys livin' on their backs, or in their wheelchairs, over at the VA hospital. I get to come and go as I please, and I get to breathe the air of a free man. Like a lot of other guys, I fought for that right and mean to take advantage of it until the day I die. No sponging off the government and whining about not gettin' enough handouts. No, siree ... not me.

But I'm rambling. You'll have to forgive me; at my age I guess rambling comes with the territory. Anyhow, I was fixin' to tell you about something wonderful. It happened to me just the other week. I was sitting here reading one afternoon when all of a sudden I hear scratching at my door, along with a gentle "Woof." When I opened the door, there was the purtiest white dog you ever saw. He was full-grown—heck, his head looked my belt buckle right in the eye. He had short, shiny hair, and smelled like he just had a bath, too.

Well, sir, this dog shows up and drops an old baseball right at my feet ... uh ... foot. Before I could say a word, he kneeled down—you know how they squat down on their front paws with their butts in the air when they want to play? I tell you, my heart melted right into a puddle. I sat down in front of him and began stroking his chin, trying to get acquainted. Before I knew it, he was lickin' my face like we'd been friends all our lives.

After we got done introducin' ourselves, he picked up his ball and curled up in front of the fire like he was kin. I had the feeling he could tell I wasn't up for any runnin'-around games.

When it came dinner time, I rummaged around in my kitchen for something to offer him, but all I could find was some crackers and cheese. He scarfed it up, though, and then sat down in front of me and put his head in my lap. I scratched his head and told him he could stay the night and we'd go out a-huntin' his owners in the morning. He didn't have a collar, but I figgered a purty dog like him must be owned by somebody who cared.

And that's what we did. The next day, after Dog—that's what I started calling him—and I did our business and ate some cheese and crackers, we started out to find his family. Funny thing, though. He wasn't having any of it. Every few yards, he'd just sit down on the path and whine. I told him all about the wonderful things that would happen when we found his owners, but he still wasn't interested.

Then, when I turned around to look back at my shack, Dog perked up and ran straight for my door. I followed behind, of course, but when I didn't hobble fast enough, he tugged at my pant leg to hurry me along. If'n I didn't have my crutch to help me balance, I might have fallen flat on my butt. When we got back to the shack, he put his paws up on the door and said, "Ruff." I was sure he was trying to get me to hurry and open up. When I did, he ran right in, slurped a drink of water from the bowl I'd put down for him, and then curled up in front of the fireplace.

It was like he was tellin' me that *this* was his place and we didn't need to go lookin' for another. Well, I was really touched by that. Good thing we were alone, cause I wouldn't'a wanted anyone to see the tear slidin' down my cheek.

So we spent the day playin' ball—I'd toss it and he'd bring it back. But here's another funny thing. He didn't drop the ball at my foot. He put it right in my hand so I wouldn't have to bend over for it. That was pretty special, and I wondered if he'd been trained to care for invalids.

The next day brought more surprises. When I let Dog out for a morning run, he didn't come back. I was sad about that, thinkin' he was gone for good. He had brought a lot of love and smiles into my simple life in just one day and I would miss him. I moped around all morning wondering if I should go out and look for him. He was only gone a few hours, but I already missed him pretty bad.

Much to my surprise, after getting up from my afternoon nap, I heard a muffled bark at the door. I knew right away it was Dog, and my spirits soared. "Coming," I said, and hobbled to the door as fast as I could which, of course, wasn't very fast. When I opened the door, there he was, his tail waggin' so hard I thought he might shake his butt off. He walked in as though he owned the place and I told him he was welcome. But he didn't head for the fireplace. He sat down in front of me and held up the brown paper bag he carried in his mouth. I was so happy he was back, I guess I didn't notice that before. I had no idea what that was about. I thought maybe he'd swiped a lunch from one of the construction workers down there by the saw mill. After taking a closer look at my "gift," I thought the bag didn't look crumpled enough for a construction worker to be hauling around.

"Well, now," I said, "what do we have here?"

He didn't say anything, just kept waggin' his tail and pushing the bag at my hand. So I took it and looked inside. It was somebody's lunch, all right. Three ham sandwiches, some pickles, a couple of shiny apples and a doughnut. They were a welcome sight, but I wondered how Dog came by such a good-smellin' feast.

I asked him where he got it, figgerin' somebody would soon come bangin' on my door wantin' his lunch back. Dog didn't say anything, of course. But he didn't look guilty, neither, when I asked him if he stole it. Just sat there with a big grin on his face. So it was a mystery. Now don't get me wrong—it was definitely a welcome surprise, but it was a mystery even so.

That night we ate in style, and when we were done fillin' our bellies, we both curled up by the fireplace like two contented pigs. I put an arm over his shoulder and he lifted his head and licked my face. Life was sweet.

The next morning, Dog was ready to go out, way before I was ready to think about breakfast, so I opened the door. He sniffed around until he found a few prime places to pee, then headed off down the path at a trot. I couldn't help wonderin' if he was gonna filch another lunch-bag someplace. By now, though, I was pretty sure he'd come back, so I hobbled down to the general store at the crossroads to stock up on a few things, including something for my new friend.

Sure enough, he was back by the middle of the afternoon. I stood on the porch watchin' him strut up the path, head held high—with another brown bag in his mouth. He sat in front of me and handed me the bag, looking very proud of himself.

"All right," I said, scratching him under the chin, "Let's go inside and see what you swiped for us today." By then, y'see, I guess I took it for granted he'd found himself a prime place to steal fresh food. Didn't make much sense the food was already made into sandwiches and neatly wrapped in wax paper. But why look a gift lunch in the— well, you know what I mean.

We hustled inside and I spread the bag contents on the table. This time, in addition to the sandwiches and things, there was a piece of cherry pie in a plastic container. It looked like real pie, too, not the store-bought kind. And it smelled so good I almost dug into it even before it got to be dinner time. I rummaged through the sack some more, to see if there was some kind of note, but couldn't find any.

The next two days was more of the same. I let Dog out for his morning adventure like I always did, thinkin' I was the luckiest guy alive to have a friend like him. He trotted off down the path like he always did, stoppin' off here and there to leave a message tellin' the other dogs in the neighborhood he'd been by.

But the next day was different. A lot different. I no sooner got settled in with a book I was readin' when Dog was back, scratchin' at the door and barking for all he was worth. Real agitated is what he was. Naturally, I hurried to find out what the fuss was about. When I opened the door, he barked a couple of times to let me know he was serious, and then started tuggin' at my pant leg. He let go for a few seconds to bark some more, then tugged at me again. Didn't take me long to figure out he wanted me to follow him and be quick about it.

"Okay," I said, "just let me close the door and we'll go." We started out. He ran ahead and then back to me to find out why I wasn't moving as fast as he was. Back and forth, barking like there was no tomorrow.

About the time I was running out of steam, he tugged me off the path onto a graveled walkway that led to a little house. Not a shack like mine, but a real house. It was small, but it was a real house with real glass in the windows and—stuff like that. As I hobbled up the two steps to the front door, I noticed it was open a crack and decided to peek in. But darned if Dog didn't get up on his hind legs and push the door wide open.

I felt pretty squeamish about walking into somebody's house like that, but I did. "Hello. Anybody home?" I called. But there was no answer. Dog tugged me toward another room and I called out again. Again no response. But I saw a pair of legs on the floor and rushed in to see what had happened. The legs belonged to a woman—somewhere around my age, I guessed— lying on her back and out cold. I balanced myself on my one knee and felt for the woman's pulse. I wasn't a stranger at that sort of thing—the war taught me about first aid.

The faint pulse in her neck told me she was still alive, so I looked her over to see if she was bleedin' someplace. She wasn't, and I couldn't find any other reason she should be unconscious. Just then Dog started pokin' at me. When I looked in his direction he dropped one of those medical alert things on the floor right next to me. You know, one of those things you hang around your neck so you can call somebody in an emergency. Well, this was an emergency, all right, so I pressed the button a few times, hopin' there was somebody on the other end to hear. While I was pressing the button, Dog went back to lickin' the lady's face like it was covered with steak sauce.

I couldn't just kneel there doing nothing while Dog did all the work, so I leaned over her and started givin' her CPR. It was a long time since I'd done that, and I hoped I was close to doin' it right. So I just kept on as best I could. I had to push Dog's face out of the way each time I needed to pump in a few breaths, but then he'd nudge mine out of the way when he thought it was his turn to lick some more.

Just about the time my back started givin' out, I heard sirens up on the road behind the house. "Dog," I said, "go bring them down here." He didn't need to be told twice, and scampered out the door and up the rise. Wasn't long before I heard his bark, along with the sound of men talking. When I heard footsteps on the porch I hollered for them to come to the bedroom. They did, and took over the job pretty quick.

"Do you know what happened to her?" the medics asked as they worked. I told them I didn't. "Actually, I was at home reading my book when Dog here came and got me. When I couldn't find any bleeding, I cleared her throat and started CPR."

When Dog went back to lickin' her face, she came around and smiled. "Good Doody," she managed to say, and I guessed "Doody" was Dog's real name.

The medics did their thing and then put her on a stretcher. They carried her to the ambulance with me and Dog trailing behind. They didn't want to let us ride along, but Dog wouldn't hear of it. He put up such a fuss, they finally gave in and we climbed aboard. You might have thought Dog was a trained doctor the way he watched every move they made on the way to the hospital. If'n they didn't tell him what they was about to do to her, he'd "Ruff" a little and paw at their butts to remind them.

Well, it all worked out. Lila—that's her name—had had a little heart attack and now takes a bit of medication to keep from gettin' another one. Dog and I stayed by her bed for the two days she took to recover—Dog got pretty mean when anybody tried to chase us away.

Lila is okay now. She still sends Dog over with a lunch bag, and we have dinner together twice a week at her house. But we're thinking of upping that to three, because that seems to make Dog real happy. Okay, I'll admit it—it does wonderful things for my disposition, too.

Of course, Dog manages to nudge himself into the middle of things. He doesn't waste any time at all when he sees a lap to crawl onto, or a knee to put his head on. But he's happiest when he can snuggle up between us when we're sittin' on the couch watchin' TV. That way he can get scratched by two hands at the same time.

Life is sweet.

LaVergne, TN USA
03 December 2009
165731LV00001B/3/P

9 781449 035372